CHRISTMAS CHANCE

Amber Ghe

Hustle & Write Publishing

ISBN-13: 9798559059938

Cover design by: Amber Ghe
Editing: Reflected Gifts
Printed in the United States of America

This book is dedicated to those who have
rooted for Chance and True. Thank You!

To: Arlena Gordon Dean
Thank you so much FOR
your support As AN upcoming
Author it is greatly
Appreciated.
" Happy Holidays "
" Amber Yhe "
2020

CHRISTMAS CHANCE

CHRISTMAS CHANCE

Chapter One

CHANCE

It was the first of December. Even though my baby was due on Christmas Eve, I felt like I could drop at any moment. I was miserable in my skin and desperately wanted to wear a regular pair of jeans. I sauntered over to the refrigerator, knowing I didn't need to stick anything else in my mouth. I could feel my eyes welling with tears. I closed the refrigerator door and cried. I missed being able to do construction so much. But worksites were dangerous, and True didn't want me doing any hands-on jobs.

I felt like the biggest Grinch ever. I could hear my husband coming to the kitchen. I tried to pull myself together.

"Good morning, babe," I heard him say.

"Good morning," I gurgled. I knew instantly he would suspect I was crying.

"What's wrong?" He said, dropping his briefcase and jacket to the floor. "Are you in pain? Is the baby okay?" He questioned.

"Yes, I'm fine," I lied.

"Then, why are you crying?" He asked, pulling me in for a hug.

"I don't know why I'm crying. I'm just over this whole pregnancy thing already," I blurted out.

"Babe, it's almost over, and our little bundle of joy will be here," he said, kissing me on my forehead. "I have to get going. Are you going to be okay?"

"I'll be fine," I sulked. Once True left for work, I made myself a piece of toast. I didn't have much time myself before I had to be at work. I headed upstairs to shower and pull myself together. I was actually looking forward to going to work. It was a great escape from this baby that was taking over my life. I put on a little makeup and a cute dress and swept my unruly hair up into a top knot. I grabbed my coffee mug and headed out the door. I stopped and grabbed donuts for the office, which were secretly for me. I had to keep the baby happy so I could get some work done.

"Good morning," I said to everyone who beat me to work.

"Good morning," I heard them repeat back.

"Good morning, best friend. Don't you look gorgeous today," Chelle commented.

"Now, you know you don't have to give me compliments in order to get your Christmas bonus," I joked.

"Nah, Sis, I'm serious. You really look good. You were in such great shape before your pregnancy that you barely look pregnant," Chelle said.

She was laying it on real thick this morning. I hugged her. "Thanks," I said. I did need the compliment. I felt like I was in unchartered waters with this pregnancy.

I tried to put a little pep in my step, but I felt the wobble taking over no matter how I tried. I dropped my coat and purse off in my office and headed to the breakroom with the donuts. I was ready for our nine o'clock meeting. I grabbed the best-looking donut and got started, so I could get myself together before everyone piled in.

"Great! Now that we're all here, it's time to re-evaluate

the end of year numbers and whether or not we need to hire more staff. Do you guys think the office will be okay when I'm out on maternity leave because I can have True and William oversee the construction side of things?" I questioned.

"Chance, you know my section is cool. Kelvin and I have things under control," Chelle responded.

"I think it would be a good idea if True and William support the construction side while you're gone. That way, I don't fall behind with the special orders," Zen stated.

"Okay, that won't be a problem. Plus, I can do some stuff from home as long as everyone keeps me in the loop," I replied.

I noticed how Chelle and Zen couldn't keep their eyes off each other, and it tickled me inside. She'd better mind her business before she ended up looking like me.

"Okay, which one of you wants to be in charge of putting together a holiday party?" I asked.

"I'll do it," Kelvin chimed in. "Now ya'll know I can throw a party."

"Yeah, he's right about that," Chelle concurred.

"Great! Kelvin, try to give us the details at the end of the week since we don't have much time before the holidays," I suggested.

"Will do," he replied.

I grabbed another donut before getting up.

"Pretend ya'll didn't see that," I giggled.

Everyone headed to their workspaces. My workload was actually light because during the winter in Ohio, the frozen ground put a halt to most construction jobs. I sat down at my desk and picked up the purchase order Chelle left and went over everything line by line. Everything was on point. We did well following our budget this year. Chelle tapped on my door.

"Come in."

"Hey girl, how are you feeling?" she asked. " I see your smile, but it's not reaching your eyes. What's really going on?"

I sighed. "Christmas for me is hard. It used to be me and my daddy's favorite holiday when I was little. He always let me open one gift on Christmas eve. And now, my baby is due on Christmas Eve, and my dad won't be there to see my baby being born."

Chelle got up and rubbed my back.

"Aw, sweetie, I know you miss your dad. I miss him, too. I remember he would take us to the drive-in movies and give us all the junk food we wanted to eat," she reminisced. I giggled. Chelle made the thoughts of missing my daddy fun.

"You know your daddy is with you. Why do you think your baby is due on Christmas Eve? You don't think that's a coincidence, do you?" She asked.

"I never thought of it that way."

"You are getting a real live present for Christmas," Chelle smiled, still rubbing my back.

Best friends always had a way of making you feel better when you needed the extra push.

"Thanks, girl."

"No problem. Everything I said is the truth. Plus, I'm ready to be an Auntie."

We laughed.

"Girl, aren't we supposed to be meeting with Trinity for lunch today?" Chelle asked.

"Oh, that's right. We better get going. You're driving," I said.

"As long as you don't mind riding in the Pinto," she

laughed.

"You're a fool! That is not a Pinto."

"I'm just saying."

I locked my computer and grabbed my coat and purse while I waited on Chelle. After the donuts you'd think I wouldn't be hungry, but nope. I was ready for some real food. I followed Chelle to her car, which was not a Pinto like she called it. But she'd definitely put a beating on the poor car.

Once we were seated at our favorite table, Chelle waved to Trinity, standing at the door, perusing the crowd. She saw us and headed our way.

"What's up?" Trinity asked.

"Girl, how are you going to invite us to lunch and then be late," Chelle laughed.

Trinity bent down and gave us hugs.

"I ain't thinking about you!" Trinity laughed.

"Hey, Trin," I chimed in.

"You guys are looking lovely today," Trinity commented.

"Thanks," Chelle stated truthfully.

"Thanks for coming. I actually invited you guys here because I wanted to ask you two to be my bridesmaids," Trinity smiled.

"Yes, of course," Chelle and I beamed.

Chapter Two

TRUE

I was happy I beat my wife home from work. I would fix a nice meal to give her time to put her feet up and relax. I washed my hands and got busy by pulling chicken breast out of the fridge. I seasoned it really well and put it in the oven. Next, I fried potatoes, onions, and green peppers and made green beans. I had to admit I had the house smelling good. When my baby walked through the door, I immediately grabbed her coat and led her into the kitchen.

Hey babe," I greeted my wife with a kiss.

"Hey, ooooh, it smells delicious."

"Wash your hands and let's sit down and eat," I said. "So, how was your day?"

"Mmmm," she moaned before answering, "It was pretty good. Everyone voted that you and William oversee the construction side of things while I'm on maternity leave."

"Oh, okay, that sounds good. Luckily this is the slow season. I know your business was booming a couple of months ago."

"Exactly, I think that's going to be our only savior," Chance agreed.

"Kelvin volunteered to put together a holiday party. Of course, you and William are a part of our team. You'll be expected to participate," she said.

"I'm sure that won't be a problem for William. You know I'm down," I replied, digging into my food. "Now that we have all the business out of the way, are you going to tell me what was wrong this morning?"

"I really can't tell you because I was in my emotions. One thing I do know is I'm ready for this pregnancy to be over. And I'm missing my daddy. Christmas used to be our favorite holiday," she said.

I was at a loss for words. I knew she was going through something, but I didn't know how to fix it.

"Come on, babe," I said, reaching for her hand. I led her into the family room, settled on the couch, and kicked up her feet. I sat down at the end of the couch and rubbed them. I rubbed her feet, ankles, and calves. I could tell by the look on her face she loved every bit of the attention I was giving.

"So, have you thought of any more names for the baby?" I asked.

"No," she moaned at the motions I was putting on her feet.

"Well, we need to come up with something before our bundle of joy gets here."

"Yeah, you're right. What do you have in mind?" Chance asked.

"I don't know, True Jr.," I laughed.

"I know. We could combine our names and name our child, Trance." She giggled even though I kind of liked that name.

"What do you want, a boy or a girl?" I asked.

"Boy, because I don't know how I feel about having to do hair, you know," she commented. "What about you?" She asked.

"You know every man's dream is to have a little shorty, but then again, I would love to have a sweet baby girl to love on, too." I smiled at my wife. She was so beautiful. But

I had hurt her too many times. She didn't have that grit and flair like she did when we first got together. I was childish in so many ways, and I took for granted that she'd always be by my side. I stood up and walked over to the window. I was kind of messed up myself knowing I hurt her. I also wondered if she'd ever be that woman I first met? Or if I caused her to bury that girl a long time ago. I walked back over to the couch.

"Babe, Babe, I just wanted to say I'm sorry. I know you've heard those words too many times from me. But I want to thank you for having my baby. Without my parents or brother, I have been a lost soul for years. It wasn't that I didn't love you. I didn't know how to love. I know how to sex a woman and then go on about my business. I didn't know how to become a permanent fixture in someone's life. But having this baby gives me more insight into what it means to show up every day for my family," I said. Tonight, there were no shadows across my heart. I got down on my knees and laid my head across her lap. I was giving her pure vulnerability.

"I love you. Thanks for telling me how you feel because you know all I could think about is the next time you'll mess me over." She sat back, momentarily rebuffed. "Honestly, I wondered if that was a part of where my tears came from. The unknown of where I stand in your life and always wondering if someone like Solace Black will come along and take my place." She shrugged to hide her confusion.

"Like I said"—

"As you've said before," she cut me off.

"Look, I'm not trying to start a fight. I was just being real with you, something I hadn't done. I can admit, before I was appeasing to the moment. But this is coming from right here." I pounded my chest. I moved my mouth over hers, devouring its softness. Her eyes were filled with a deep curious longing.

"Babe, let's do this for our baby. Let's recommit to why we got together in the first place. Let's rewind to the night when we met at the fight party. Okay, hold on, I was across the room standing next to Kelvin while the fight was going on. I was on the phone with William." I walked across the room and pulled my cell phone out of my pocket. "Yeah, Will, I heard a beautiful woman put in a bid for a job with our company. Of course, I'm open-minded. Let me look at her bid at work tomorrow. Right now, I'm trying to watch this fight, and there's this fine ass babe all in my mouth. Dang Kelvin, I missed the TKO trying to peep this fine honey across the room." We busted out laughing.

Chance got off the couch. "Yooo, Chelle, who's ole boy over there with the cocoa brown skin, and deep dimples? Girl, I don't know, but he's fine. You want me to get his name?" Chance mimicked Chelle. "Nah, I'm ready to go home, but I'll probably see him jogging in the park tomorrow." We laughed again.

With that belly, Chance was trying to stretch. "Then I heard this deep falsetto behind me like, 'I remember you from the fight party last night. Do you come here often?'"

I shook my head. I laughed at her imitation of me, especially with the perfectly round belly sitting in front of her.

I took over the demonstration. "Then we saw each other again at Cornbread Fred's. That was the first time I slept over at your place. I was a gentleman, but I should have hit way back then." We laughed again.

"Yeah, this is the part we need to rewrite, when you messed around with Solace because I didn't let you hit it from behind." She turned around and kicked her leg up while trying to twerk. I cringed because it was so comical looking but still sexy. Her breasts were full, and her behind was nice and plump. I bit down on my bottom lip. My feelings for her intensified as my seed grew in her belly.

Chapter Three

CHANCE

The look on his face mingled eagerness with tenderness. It was a look of admiration, which was not something I received from True often. His fingers wrapped around the dark fabric of my sleeve as he pulled me into the crevice of his chest. The tantalizing scent of his aftershave made me swoon.

"You know you're truly an amazing woman, don't you?"

"Where is this coming from?" I asked.

"I can't help but wonder how you've put up with me and my childish ways. It takes an amazing person to put up with everything I put you through."

I sighed. "Thanks, but I don't know. There is not much more room for error, sir. In fact, you will need to go some years without a glitch before you gain another life," I laughed.

"Gain another life, hun?" True threw his head back and laughed. "You are the epitome of what Ride or Die defines. Thank, you for not giving up on me," True mumbled into my hair.

"Let's watch a movie, babe," I said to my sexy husband.

"Okay. I'll grab some snacks while you put your feet up. Find us something good," True added, heading to the kitchen.

I sat down and grabbed the remote control, smitten by the attention I was finally getting from my husband. I could get used to this. But the way I was set up caused me to be guarded at all times. I had been hurt too many times. I think that was one reason I got into the construction industry because I always wanted to prove I was a baddie despite wearing my heart on my sleeve. I never wanted to depend on a man. All the men I'd been around were unreliable, yeah, even my father. That didn't make me love him any less. It just led me to believe all men had those untrustworthy tendencies. Honestly, sometimes I wondered what I was even doing here.

"I got snacks," True sang, interrupting my thoughts.

"Come on through, Mr. Fourlove," I joked. Once the snacks were gone, I fell asleep and let the movie watch me. I woke up to True carrying me to the bedroom. Undressing me, True tucked me into bed. He climbed in behind me, rubbing my belly and my swollen breast. I felt his manhood grow.

"Babe, can I make love to you? I promise I'll be gentle," True asked in-between kisses.

"Mmmm, yes, I want you," I moaned as he spread my legs. I felt an eager affection coming from him. As he entered, he struck a vibrant chord inside me. Our melodic rhythm matched our heavy breaths when his eyes caught and held mine.

"I love you," he yelled at the pinnacle moment.

"Ohhh shiiii, I love you, too." I came so hard. I was so wet I thought my water had broken.

"Damn girl, that was good," True huffed.

"Yes, it was. I'm going to take a quick shower, babe." I climbed out of bed. In the shower, I thanked God for allowing me to live the beautiful life I deserved. I dried off and put on a pair of panties and a t-shirt. I climbed back in bed next to my man. He draped his arm around me and held me tight all night long.

The next morning, I looked at the clock. It was ten-thirty. I needed to get my day started. I was going to have lunch with the girls and maybe do some light Christmas shopping. I climbed out of bed, and immediately felt something.

"Oooh," I yelped.

"What's wrong, babe?" True asked.

"I had a little cramping. I'm okay. It was probably from the sex last night," I assured him.

"Lay back down," he suggested.

"No, I'm okay. I have a few errands to run today."

"Okay, well, don't overdo it. I guess I need to get up and get a move on, too."

He rolled over, got out of the bed, and stretched. My husband's handsome features had always smitten me. After I dressed, I waited by the couch for Trinity to pick me up. I wasn't up for driving. She texted my phone telling me she was in the driveway. I put on my coat and grabbed my little crossbody bag that barely fit because of my belly and yelled out.

"Babe, I'm leaving."

"Be careful," I heard him answer.

I waddled out to Trinity's car and got in.

"Hey, girl," I said. "Thanks for picking me up."

"No problem. How are you feeling today?" Trinity asked.

"Pretty good. I'm getting excited for the holidays," I smiled.

"Me too, girl. Can you believe I'm engaged? Who knew I would ever give love a chance again after Adam?" Trinity pulled out of the driveway and headed towards Chelle's house. There was a light dusting of snow on the ground, and the neighborhoods were all decorated for the holidays.

We pulled up in front of Chelle's house and honked the horn. Chelle came out of the house and hopped into the back seat.

"Hey ya'll," she sang.

"What's up girl," I chimed. "You look cute."

"Thanks, girl," Chelle answered.

Trinity turned up the radio. "This is my jam."

Chelle snapped her fingers. "Girl, this is the cut."

They tickled me. It was so good to be with my friends.

"I think we should do a little shopping first, and then we

can eat when we get tired," I suggested.

"That sounds good," Trinity added.

"I'm cool with that," Chelle said.

"I want to go to the new outlet mall. I heard they were having a good sale," said Trinity.

"Oh yeah, they have a new Baby Depot that I want to visit," I noted.

When we pulled up to the store, we got to park in the expectant mother space in front. I was excited to see all the baby stuff. Once inside the store, all you heard was,

"This is so cute, awe, and look how little."

I picked out a few neutral things since I didn't know the sex of the baby. We went to a few other stores. Everyone was picking out stuff for their parents or significant others. I picked out a gorgeous watch for True. He was a collector of watches. In his eyes, a person could never have enough watches. I also picked out a beautiful handbag for mom, who had the same mentality. A woman could never have enough purses. By this time, we were beat and ready for lunch, which would be more like dinner according to the time.

We secured our bags in the trunk and drove around to

the other side of the building where the food court was.

"I don't want any fast food. Do you mind if we go somewhere so I can pick out something a little healthier?" I asked.

"Right," I heard Chelle say from the back seat.

Trinity kept driving down the boulevard a little farther where the better restaurants were. We decided on a nice cafeteria that had a full menu of delicious foods to choose from.

"Thanks, I'm craving fruit and veggies," I rubbed my belly.

Once we were seated with our trays of food, I started to feel better after drinking a little and giving my feet a much-needed break.

"Trinity, how's the reality show going?" Chelle asked.

"It's going well. We got picked up for a second season," Trinity beamed.

"Congratulations," Chelle and I said.

"I need to start planning this wedding soon," Trinity commented.

"Have you picked out your colors yet?" I asked.

"No, not yet. I'm still trying to figure out what kind of

wedding I want. Heck, for all I know, we might go to the justice of the peace and call it a day. You know, since we're both divorcee's the wedding just isn't that important," Trinity said.

"Girl, you may have both been down that road before, but you still need to celebrate this new love. Don't minimize what you have with each other just because you've been married before," I told her.

"Ain't that the truth," Chelle stated.

"Yeah, I've never thought about it that way. We should celebrate each other and not go into marriage worried that we're divorcees," Trinity stated.

"Or being worried that your marriage won't last because the first one didn't," Chelle added.

"Yeah," I chimed in. "I think too many people go into marriage with divorce on their minds when it shouldn't even be an option according to our vows," I added.

"We do need to be mindful of our thoughts," Trinity agreed.

"Oh my gosh, this food is so good," I said after taking a bite of my dessert.

"Girl, who eats their dessert first?"

Chelle and Trinity laughed at me.

"Don't judge me. It looked so good, I had to taste it," I commented before we all busted out laughing.

"Guys, I had a good time today. Chance, you need to have that baby before Christmas because I won't have anywhere to go for Christmas if you're in the hospital," Chelle said.

"You can come to my house, Chelle," Trinity replied.

"We'll have our Christmas early this year when we celebrate at our party," I reminded them.

"Oh yeah, I forgot. I could get cute," Chelle laughed.

Trinity said, "Girl, I got my outfit for the party. I'm going to be looking fine," she laughed.

"I think I have a nice little moo-moo I can put on for the party," I said, feeling left out.

"Girl, please. You'll be back to yourself in no time," Trinity reminded me.

"I just want to wear a pair of jeans with a button and zipper in the front."

"I can wear those, but I still like the stretchy stuff," Trinity laughed.

"Right," Chelle added. She was holding her hand up for a high five.

Chapter Four

TRUE

With Chance gone Christmas shopping with her girls, I had to act fast. I had a whole crew ready to help me set up the baby's nursery. The furniture would be delivered in a few hours. I hired the painters to paint the nursery a mint green. They also added a cute jungle mural on one wall. The furniture was whitewashed oak. The crib would convert into a toddler bed once our baby was too big for it. I ordered a large stuffed giraffe and rocking horse, a leather armchair and ottoman, and a big white plush rug. I also ordered a teepee for our child to play in once he or she got a little older. The room was very gender friendly and free-spirited like Chance. I knew she would love it.

I texted with Trinity to keep my wife away from home long enough to get everything set up. I wanted the room to be complete when she saw it because she wanted to wait until after the baby was born when we learned the baby's gender. My mother in law was gracious enough to help coordinate the furniture and accessories. I was concerned about Chance being tired once the baby was born. I didn't want her to be stressed out but able to enjoy being a new mother. I kept looking at my watch because I knew my wife would be tired early, and I needed this to go smoothly. The painters set up a massive fan in the room once they were finished to help dry the paint faster. One of the contractors was still working on the accent wall.

The doorbell rang. It was the movers with the baby furniture.

"Come on in. Let me show you where to set up," I said to the delivery man.

I showed the man the room and then signed some paperwork.

"We'll get everything pulled out and remove the plastic once we get inside," the man stated.

"Sounds good," I told him.

"I'm finished with the mural, Mr. Fourlove," the lady who'd been painting told me.

"Great, let's go look at it."

When we got to the room, the image was spot on. This mural is freaking awesome," I told her. "My wife is going to love this."

I gave the lady a fist bump.

"I'm so glad you love it. We'll get this fan out of your way. Make sure to tell the movers to be careful not to touch the walls," she advised.

"Will do. Thank you so much."

We headed to the door where she asked her coworker to grab the giant fan. I motioned for the head guy from the moving truck to come over.

"Hey, my man, they just finished painting the walls in the room. Please advise your crew to be careful when moving the furniture in."

"Got it, thanks for letting me know. I'll tell the crew. We have everything ready to bring in," the moving guy told me.

"Great, let's get it. I'm pressed for time," I commented, looking at my watch.

Minutes later, they were setting up the furniture, and then the room would be complete. Once Chance and I came up with a name for our baby, I would order the letters to be placed on the crib's wall.

I let the delivery guys out the front door and locked it behind them. I texted Trinity that the room was complete.

She texted back that Chance was getting tired, and she would drop her off soon. I walked into the completed room and almost buckled at the knees at the fantastic job. This might be the best present I'd ever given my wife. I walked over to the leather pecan brown armchair and propped up the fluffy white pillow. I picked up my cell phone and called my mother in law.

"Hey, mom, it's done."

"Oooh, how does it look?" She asked.

"The painters did an amazing job. This room will be perfect for a girl or boy. I'm sure Chance is going to love it," I told her.

"I'm so happy. This will take a huge load off her shoulders," Mom added.

"Right. I'm so glad you helped me pull this off. Thanks again."

"Oh, you're more than welcome. Anything for my babies," Mom commented.

"Well, let me get off here. Don't forget to come by tomorrow at two for the photoshoot," I reminded her.

"I'll be there, mmn bye," she said before hanging up.

I ended the call and turned out the light on my way out the door. I walked into the living room in time to see Trinity's car pull into the driveway. I opened the front door when I noticed the trunk popped open. *This girl done bought a lot of stuff*, I said to myself. I slipped on my shoes and jogged out to the car to help with the packages.

"Go on in the house, baby. I got this," I said, heading to the trunk.

"Bye, ladies," Chance said while waving.

"Hey, Brother-in-law. How did everything go?" Trinity asked once Chance was out of earshot.

"Perfect. You guys can come for the photoshoot tomorrow at two," I told her as she handed me Chance's packages.

"I'll be here for sure, and I'll remind Chelle," Trinity stated.

"Thanks again for helping out," I told her. Trinity jumped in her car, and I waved at her and Chelle before heading into the house.

"Babe, did you buy the store," I joked.

She giggled. "Just put that stuff in the guest room and don't be looking in the bags," she called out.

When I came back, she had curled up on the couch, looking so comfortable.

"Babe, I gotta show you something," I reached out for her hands.

"Awe, man, I don't want to move," Chance said.

"I know, but you really need to come see this."

I used my strength to help pull her up off the couch. I led her to the nursery and opened the door turning on the light. I watched Chance's mouth fall open, then she covered her mouth with her hands.

"Oh my God," she exclaimed before the tears took over.

"Do you like it?"

"Of course, it's beyond beautiful," she cried.

"Once we pick out the baby's name, we can get his or her name put on the wall over the crib," I explained. I led her to the leather armchair. "You can sit here and rock the baby at night," I said, running around the room, showing her everything.

"This is absolutely gorgeous, and I like that it's for a girl or boy," Chance said. "Thanks, True, this is so beautiful."

"Anything for you, babe. Now you need to get ready for bed or layout and relax for a while because we are having a photoshoot tomorrow, and our friends and family are coming to watch."

"Oh my gosh, I'm so excited. But yes, I'm exhausted. I want to take a quick shower and get into something comfortable and chill the rest of the evening. Oh yeah, and I did bring you a to-go plate because I knew I wasn't cooking anything after being on my feet all day," she commented.

"Awe, thanks for thinking about me, babe. I haven't had time to eat a thing today, trying to coordinate everything to pull this off," I told her.

I turned off the lights in the nursery and followed Chance to the bedroom.

"Go ahead and eat while I take a quick shower. I'll meet you in the theatre room," she said.

"Okay." I headed to the kitchen. My baby had brought me a ribeye steak, baked potato, and corn on the cob that I put on a plate and heated in the microwave. I was all too happy to have pulled everything off. And now that I'd eaten something, I was tired, too. I grabbed two bottles of water and headed to the theatre room to snuggle with my baby. She was already sleeping. I sat down on the chaise next to Chance and got under the blanket. I watched TV for all of five minutes before falling asleep next to my wife.

Chapter Five

CHANCE

I opened my eyes to the bright sun flowing through the windows. I slept so well after being on my feet most of yesterday. I climbed out of bed without waking my husband. I felt like I had been dreaming when I thought about the baby's nursery, so I had to go make sure I wasn't.

I opened the door to the nursery, and my mouth dropped open again. I could not believe how cute the room was. I walked around and examined all the goodies, and now instead of dread, I felt the life growing inside of me as a being and not something that was going to ruin my life. I walked over to the guest room and grabbed the bags of baby stuff I'd purchased. I was excited to hang the little clothes in the closet and put the cute little trinkets on the dressers. I noticed True added the diapers and some of the stuff from the baby shower. I picked up a book off the bookshelf and sat down in the comfy armchair.

I opened the book and smiled at the endearing photos.

"There you are," True said.

"Good morning, baby," I beamed. "I thought I was dreaming about this room, so I had to confirm it was real," I laughed.

"Yeah, it's real," True repeated.

He sat down on the plush rug.

"This is nice. Feel it," he said.

I took my barefoot and ran it over the carpet. "It is soft," I agreed.

"You know I don't talk about my parents too much, but somehow, now that our baby is going to be born, I keep thinking about them, especially my mom. I remember one time when my brother and I were little boys. Our parents were so broke. They tried hard to hide it from us, but I knew. My father was having a hard time keeping a job, so my mother took her retirement money and gave it to my dad to start his business. But you know how, when you start a business, you're in the red for years before you can turn a profit? We were all petrified that if his business flopped, we would lose everything. My mother, bless her heart, backed him in every way. I think that's why I admire her so much. She was the epitome of what a woman should be."

I couldn't help but cringe a little when he described how much he admired his mom, only because I wished I could live up to her standards. True was quiet for a minute.

"This one Christmas, I was terrified we wouldn't get anything just because I'd always heard how my parents talked about not having any money to pay the bills. I knew deep down there wasn't a Santa Clause. Still, it hurt deep that my brother and I would get up and not have anything under the tree. Mentally I'd prepared myself by trying to get in trouble. I thought that if I were a bad boy, they wouldn't feel too bad for not providing our Christmas.

"True that was so selfless of you," I commented.

"Yeah, but I put my parents through the wringer that year. They kept giving me chance after chance until right before Christmas vacation. My teacher wrote a note to my mother about how bad I'd been in school. I took the sealed note home to my mother, happy that I'd accomplished my mission. But when I saw the hurt on my mother's face, I felt horrible.

"Boy, your father and I work too hard for you to be acting up like this in school," Mom fussed.

"But then she full-on started crying, and that hurt me to my core. I never wanted to make my mother cry. I was only trying to get her out of having to explain why we wouldn't have Christmas," True sighed as he looked down.

"What happened?"

"Well, once I saw mom crying, I blurted out, 'Mom, I did it for you. I only got in trouble because I didn't want you to feel bad for not giving me a Christmas.' I cried, too. She had a stunned look on her face. My mom opened her arms, and I fell into her embrace. Then she said, 'True, that was not for you or your brother to worry about. All you had to do was be a child, a good child,' she smiled at me. I'll never forget the way she looked at me that day. Her image is burned into my memory," True admitted.

"Awe," I said quietly.

"Anyway, on Christmas morning, my brother woke me up and told me to come on. We headed to the living room. Low and behold, the presents were packed under the tree. My brother looked at me, and I looked at him before we said, 'Oh my God look at all the presents.' We ran to the tree and grabbed the boxes. It was the most memorable Christmas ever. But I remember looking over, and my mother was standing there watching my brother and me. The expression on her face was priceless.

"One thing I don't ever want for our child is to be worried about our finances. Even if we're flat broke, I never want my child to worry about adult stuff," True said.

"You're right about that. It's hard because children are smart. They know when things aren't right with their parents," I shook my head. My husband was finally opening up to me and revealing things I knew he'd never shared with anyone else. He was so vulnerable in that moment. It made me love him even more. I was in love with this side of him.

"I can't help but think how happy she'd be having a grandchild," True lamented.

I rubbed his shoulder. "I know it's gotta be hard. I can't imagine not having at least one parent," I told him.

"It just dawned on me that other than you, I'm alone in this world. I mean, of course, I have a few distant relatives but not anyone I can share my accomplishments with. I'm all in when it comes to you and our child. I'm tired of the old me with the player ways," True poured his heart out. I felt like he was truthful this time. I also hoped he wasn't just in it for the moment and that once all the newness of having a baby wore off, he would betray me again.

The old me wanted to worry about the bad things that could happen, but this time it didn't hit me that way. I had to be healthy for my baby at all costs and prayed that True fell in line.

"I can't believe you thought to have a photoshoot done today. What am I going to wear?" I asked.

"Don't worry. I got you covered. The photos will be taken here as we unveil the nursery to our family and friends. We're going to dress like we're painting the mural. It's going to be sexy," he admitted giving me all baritone.

"Oh, that sounds too cute," I admitted. True reached for my hand and helped pull me to my feet. He led me to our bedroom to show me the painters pants he would wear and the linen colored skirt I would wear with the matching bralette. He must have sensed the worry on my face about not being covered up.

"Babe, it's a pregnancy photo shoot. They are going to want to see your beautiful belly," he told me.

"I guess," I shrugged.

"Trinity is coming over to do your hair and makeup. So, don't trip," he said.

"Awe baby, I'm super excited. Thank you so much."

I stood up on my tippy toes and cupped his face before placing a sensual kiss on his lips. We ravished each other intensely. I knew I had to stop him, or we'd be running late to our own event.

"Let's get something to eat so I can have time to digest the food and get ready for this photoshoot," I advised.

"Sounds good, babe." He followed with another kiss on my forehead and tap on the butt. "But later, you're all mine."

Chapter Six

TRUE

Our morning flew by quickly, and I was excited to get everything going. I dressed in the off-white painter pants and a fresh white tee. I brushed my hair until my waves were popping. I heard the doorbell ring.

"I'll get it," I called out to Chance.

"Trinity, hey, you're right on time," I said, hugging her.

"Where is she?" She asked.

"Go on back in our room." I followed her to finish getting myself together.

"Trinity," Chance sang.

"Girl, let's get this makeup and hair beat," Trinity stated.

Chance had a robe on over her outfit. I went out of the room to straighten up the rest of the house. Next, my mother in law and Chelle came. They brought in trays of wings and veggies. My stomach growled at the sight of the delicious food.

"Hi Mom," I said, giving her a hug and kiss on the cheek after I'd taken the tray of wings off her hands.

"Hey, True. Where's my daughter?"

"Oh, she's back there getting her hair and makeup done," I answered.

"What's up, Chelle?" I hugged her, too.

"Hey brother," Chelle said. Earlier, I said I didn't have any family, but honestly, I gained two sisters and a mother when I married Chance. They all took me under their wings despite my shortfalls. Next, the people from the magazine came. I led them to the nursery to set up the lighting. Everyone who entered the room gasped when they saw the space.

"Isn't this gorgeous?" The female photographer smiled.

"Thank you," I told her. She had one other person with her who carried in a large ring light. They had a big backdrop thing they laid over the rug before putting the equipment down. I stepped out of the room to give them space to work. I went back into the kitchen and noticed William and Steal had arrived.

"Hey, True, is there anything I can do to help?" Steal asked. I looked over at Chance's mother, and she took the cue.

"Come on, baby. You can help me set the food up," Mom told her.

"Okay great," Steal said.

"Yooo Will, man, you can help me take these fold-up chairs into the nursery."

We grabbed the chairs and headed that way.

"Thanks for the invite, man."

"Most definitely. You know you had to be here," I answered.

"Is everything ready?" Trinity asked. "Chance is ready."

"Yes, we're ready," the photographer clarified.

Everyone took a seat in the nursery. When Chance walked in, I could hear the gasps.

"Awe, Chance, you look beautiful," Chelle declared.

I looked at my wife, and she glowed. Chance had never looked sexier and more scrumptious as she did carrying my baby. She walked over to me, and I embraced and kissed her, momentarily forgetting we had a crowd watching.

The photographer instructed us on different poses. My

favorite was when I sat next to the paint pallet, and Chance was next to me. I wrapped my arm around her belly and kissed it. It was such a surreal moment. We took an array of shots where I embraced her from behind and rubbed her belly, and we posed for a few others. I wasn't too bad.

"That's a wrap," the photographer said. "We got some excellent shots," she assured us.

"Thanks' for coming," I stressed.

"We should have the digital shots in your inbox tomorrow for your approval," she told me.

"Great," I answered. By this time, her coworker had the light ring packed up, and I led them to the door.

"Bye now," the lady waved.

"Bye," I told her before shutting the door.

"Let's eat," Chance's mother announced. Chance was hugging everyone and thanking them for coming to our photoshoot.

"Come on, babe, have a seat," I told Chance. Her mother handed us both plates.

I had worked up a healthy appetite. I tore those wings up.

"Have you two thought of a name for the baby yet?"

Chelle asked.

Chance shook her head no. "I'm not sure why but nothing I've heard so far sounds right to me."

"Poor nameless baby," her mother joked.

"Mom," Chance exclaimed.

"Girl, you and that son of mine better get my baby a name."

Everyone laughed.

"We're working on it," I chimed in.

"Oh, I also wanted to remind everyone about the Christmas party. We should have all the details this week on when and where it will be. I do know all the men have to wear their ugly sweaters," Chance confirmed.

"That shouldn't be too hard for William. That's all he owns is ugly sweaters." I joked.

I looked at William, and we cracked up.

"We should do some type of gift exchange, too," Steal announced.

"That would be fun," Chance commented. "I will let everyone know once I get the details from Kelvin. This party is his baby this year."

After eating, William and I sat back on the couch, and I

turned on the game. The women sat around in the kitchen, talking about everything under the sun. The living room was off the kitchen, so I ear hustled at times. The last I heard, they were talking about Trinity's wedding.

Shortly after the festivities, our guests started leaving one by one. Tomorrow was the start of the workweek, and I knew people liked to have some time to relax on Sunday evenings. I did. It was my time to get my mind right for the rigorous work week ahead.

Chance and I changed into comfortable lounge clothes. She sat down at the computer to catch up on social media while I cleaned up the kitchen.

"Babe, we got another special order for a new build," Chance noted.

"That's awesome."

"Yeah, special orders are Zen's specialty. I will remind him to reach out to you if he needs any help," she said.

"Right," I added.

"Other than that, I think everything should be good. I just want to have the baby in peace and not worry about work," Chance sighed.

"I know you do. I told you William and I got you covered.

Now, all you have to do is get my baby here safely and enjoy being a new mom," I instructed. "Now bring your sexy self in here and let me rub on that booty," I flashed my dimples at her, her soft spot!

Chapter Seven

CHANCE

I actually woke up today feeling fresh and rejuvenated. It was almost scary, but I would take advantage of this newfound energy burst and get some work done before my maternity leave started. I was the first one at work, and that hadn't happened in months.

I walked around, turning on the copiers and printers. I started up the coffee pot and brewed a fresh pot. I sat down and reviewed a job that was supposed to be completed before the year's end. Everyone trickled in a little after me. They were all surprised at my newfound energy.

"Girl, you must be nesting," Chelle commented. "It's where the mother's instinct kicks in to get everything ready before the baby is born. That baby is coming soon," Chelle advised.

"Oh my gosh, I hope so," I informed.

"Are you excited," Chelle asked.

"Yes, I still cannot believe or picture myself being a mother," I told her. Kelvin walked into my office.

"I have all the details ready for the Christmas party," Kelvin said.

"Great," I answered.

"But you need to tell everyone right away. The venue gave me a discount if we could throw the party this Thursday evening after work," he told me.

"Well, that shouldn't be a problem," I added. I picked up the handset, pressed a button, and asked Zen to join us in my office.

"Zen," I said immediately when he crossed the threshold. "Is this Thursday workable for our Christmas party?"

"The only thing I have after work right now is weightlifting. So, yeah, that works," Zen confirmed.

"I'm good with it," Chelle chimed in.

"Hold on," I said before, dialing my husband's cell phone. I tapped my pencil on the desk while waiting on him to pick up.

"Hey, babe, everything alright?" he asked. Anytime I

called him now, he immediately went into panic mode.

"I'm fine. Hey, I wanted to know if this Thursday for our Christmas party was workable for you and William?"

I heard him ask William.

"Yes, we can do it," True answered.

"Great, I'll email you the details. Make sure to tell William to tell Steal asap so she'll have a few days to get ready," I noted.

"I will," he said before hanging up the phone.

"Yes!" Kelvin announced. "I will go and wrap up the last-minute details," he added.

"Thanks," I told him.

"Chelle, will you be my date for the Christmas party?" Zen asked casually. Chelle's mouth fell open and just kind of hung there before I tapped her toes under my desk.

"I would love to," Chelle choked out.

"Great. Text me your info so I can pick you up," Zen suggested.

"I will," Chelle answered. She got up and shut my office door before we both squealed loudly.

"Oh my gosh. I haven't been on a real date in forever. I'm glad I picked out that cute party dress when we went shopping the other day," she reminded me.

"Go on, girl, with your bad self," I joked. She smiled with her beautiful white teeth. The smile came up from somewhere deep inside of her, I could tell.

"It's just an office party date. Don't turn it into something more," Chelle tried to convince me. And I gave her my best side-eye.

Days later, it was time for the Christmas party. True and I arrived early to make sure everything was on point. My hubby had on his ugly sweater, but as fine as he was, he made that ugly sweater look damn good. We both seemed to beam with pride to have each other on our arms. I had on an attractive red sequined dress that draped around my body in a flattering way. Who knew that was even possible? When I was a kid, maternity clothes were butt ugly.

The venue was a nice size. It was big enough, but also an intimate setting. Some Christmas jazz flowed through the speakers. The tables were arranged so we could all eat and talk together. The strobe light shone on the dance floor. I looked around and saw Kelvin and his significant other, Brian.

"Hey ya'll," I said. "Kelvin, you outdid yourself on this one. It looks magnificent in here," I bragged.

"Thank you, Chance. What up, True?" Kelvin and True did their chest bump handshake thing they always did. Brian and I giggled.

Chelle and Zen walked through the door, followed by William and Steal. Everyone looked gorgeous, but my friend Chelle glowed like a new woman. I'd never really noticed it before, but she and Zen made one hell of a couple.

I walked over to Steal and William. "I'm so happy you guys could make it," I told them.

"Thanks for the invite. You look so beautiful," Steal told me.

I beamed, "Awe, thanks, girl," I said.

"Chance, girl, is that even a maternity dress? You look fabulous," Chelle commented.

I giggled. "Today's maternity wear is not the maternity wear our mothers wore," I joked.

"You got that right," Steal chimed in.

Trinity and her fiancé Olympus walked in the door. They also made another good-looking couple. I thought about all of us, not too long ago, single and ready to mingle. Now look at us. The thought of it kind of melted my heart. It was funny how all the women were on one side of the room, and all the men were on the other side. When the DJ stepped up his game and played some line music, all the ladies ran to the dance floor and Kelvin and Brian because they liked to dance. We killed the steps. I wobbled for real in my little dress. Next, they played a slow jam, and all the couples hit the floor. My husband suckled my neck.

"Boy, you better be glad I'm already pregnant because the way you're kissing on me right now would surely get you a baby," I laughed.

"I can't help it. You are so sexy now that you are coming into your womanhood," True whispered in my ear. I blushed as we rocked slowly to the beat. Next, it was dinnertime, and we all gathered around the table at our designated spots marked by our name cards.

The servers brought out hot towels for our hands, followed by our salads. The main course was an excellent smothered chicken dish with roasted veggies and a dinner roll. I rubbed my belly because the baby was pleased. Once we finished with dinner, the dessert tables were set up. You could indulge in whatever fit your palate. I grabbed a sweet, decadent, something I didn't recognize. One thing I didn't do when it came to food was discriminate—especially desserts.

Kelvin went out on the dance floor with a microphone. "Okay, everyone, it's time for Christmas, Karaoke."

"Oh, nooo!" We all laughed.

"I'll start. As a matter of fact, I need my boys out here with me," he said.

William and Brian jumped up. I had to give True a little nudge before he stood up.

"Zen and O' come on bro's, you too," Kelvin coaxed.

All the women cheered them on. The Silent Night music by the Temptations played. The men laid it out like they'd rehearsed or something. They all looked fine in their ugly sweaters and slacks. True and Zen took turns on the baritone parts, while Kelvin hit the high notes. It was so damn funny. We laughed and clapped as they performed for us.

When that was over, Chelle and Trinity jumped up.

"Come on, Chance, and Steal."

We headed to the dance floor when our Christmas jam, 'What Do the Lonely Do at Christmas,' by the Emotions came on. Each one of us took turns singing the different verses, all the while giggling. We weren't on point like the men were. I think they secretly rehearsed somewhere. But each one of our men cheered us on when we took our turns singing. It was so much fun.

Next, we did the White Elephant Gift Exchange, where the first person picks a gift. The next person chooses a gift, and they get the choice to keep their gift or take some-one else's gift. To make it fair, we all drew numbers. It was hilarious because some gifts were pranks, and others were really good. Someone opened up wiener cleaner soap, which was round soap with a hole in it. The gift Chelle opened was money.

"Don't look this way. I'm keeping this money," Chelle laughed.

"How much is it?" True joked.

Brian opened up a nice bottle of liquor. The whole game was a riot. I can't remember the last time I'd laughed so hard.

"Yooo, who wants to take this Weiner Cleaner soap from me?" O' called out. "One size fits all," he joked.

"Nope, I think you're stuck with that." True and William high fived each other.

I ended up with a nice set of candles, and True ended up with a bar set. A few people danced a few more times. I was finally getting tired and ready to call it an evening. I walked around and hugged and told everyone goodbye. My husband helped me into my coat and grabbed our gifts.

Chapter Eight

TRUE

I have to admit I had a lot more fun at the party than I expected to. Everyone was in good holiday spirits, and it was a blessing to see my baby having fun despite her huge belly. I knew the pregnancy had been hard on her, but she's been a trooper. I'm blessed because of her sticking by my side. Sometimes love is right in your face, and you don't recognize it for what it is. I helped my wife into our car before getting into the other side. Thank goodness for the automatic starter. I was able to heat the car before we came outside. I had the seat warmers and steering wheel warmers going.

"You alright, babe," I asked Chance.

"Yes, I had so much fun. I think I even forgot I was pregnant for a while," she giggled.

"Did I tell you how sexy you look in that dress?"

"Yes, and thank you, but you don't have to keep flattering me," Chance looked my way.

"No, I mean it. When a woman's body changes, her breast are full, her hips spread, and her skin glows. It's an amazing process to watch as our child grows in your belly," I explained. She smiled as she laid her head back on the headrest. I could tell the car ride and heat blowing on her was allowing sleep to creep in. I reached over and grabbed her hand as I drove through the streets of Columbus, Ohio.

I pulled into our garage and hit the button to close the door behind me. I helped Chance out of the car.

"Come on, babe, we're home," I said.

"Ooooh, okay. I'm so tired," Chance mumbled.

"I know." I helped her into the house. She took her coat off and handed it to me.

"I'm so glad tomorrow's Friday because I'm beat," she told me.

"Stay home if you're tired," I advised.

"Nah, I should be okay after a full night of rest. That party just wore me out," Chance commented.

"Well, nobody told you to 'Wobble, and 'Back That

Thang Up' all night," I joked. Chance slapped me on the arm.

"Stop it," she laughed.

"Woman, you better get your behind in that bed and go to sleep before I do to you what I whispered in your ear at the party," I reminded her. Chance laughed.

"I got you this weekend, Boo. Right now, I have a date with some sheep," she joked.

I put my hand over my heart. "I'm jealous."

We turned out the lights and headed to bed.

The next morning my baby was up an at' em again. I put the pillow over my head and tried to ignore the bright lights seeping through the blinds.

"Babe, what are you doing up so early?" I mumbled from under the pillow.

"I have a lot to do today, True. I have one last job to oversee before I go on maternity leave," she explained.

"I told you I could handle it," I said, swinging my legs over the bed. *Hell, I was up now.* I thought.

"True, I don't need you to take over until I'm on maternity leave," she disputed.

"Babe, it's time for you to take it easy. I don't care what

the doctor says," I grunted mid-yawn.

"I will. I promise once I finish up these last couple of things," Chance replied. She brought me a much-needed cup of coffee then bent down and kissed me on the forehead.

"I'm off to work. It's Friday, dress down day in case you're wondering why I'm in these fat jeans," she joked. I rolled my eyes. *It was too damn early.*

The coffee gave me the boost I needed to get moving. I was getting too old to be partying on the weekday and then trying to get up and go to work the next day like I did when I was younger. I decided to go to work casual, too, by wearing a pair of khakis and a sweater. I loved Fridays because it was usually the day I went around to visit the job sites to make sure everything was on point. We also made it a point to schedule our inspections on Fridays.

I got in my car and backed out of the driveway. There wasn't a lot of snow but enough to be a nuisance. I jumped out and grabbed the shovel to hit the walkway and porch while the car finished heating up. I was so over these cold days and couldn't wait for Spring. It was slow getting to work this morning because of an accident on the freeway. I sighed. These people could not drive and panicked as soon as a little snow hit the ground.

I made it to the office. I would check in with William and update myself on the emails before heading out to the field.

"Good morning," I said to William when I walked through the door.

"What up, True," William said.

"You're here early," I commented.

"Yes, I'm ready to knock this stuff out and get my weekend started, you know, to spend a little time with my new bride," said Will.

"Yeah, I feel you," I said.

"That Christmas party was dope last night. We had a lot of fun," Will stated.

"Yeah, I actually had a good time, too," I replied.

"So, are you getting excited for your little bundle of joy?"

"You know I am. When I thought Lace's son was mine, it forced me to think in a different way. I missed the family concept. So, I'm excited for this new chapter in my life," I added.

"Yeah, I know what you mean. I've been behind the

times, even having a woman by my side. So, this is a new exciting time for both of us," William declared.

"Yes, it is," I agreed.

Chapter Nine

CHANCE

I got to work early again. I liked it because I was able to get a handle on my day without all the interruptions. Then when people started coming at me, I was ready for the challenge. I did my usual turning on the lights and such. I headed to my office to get started on my email when I noticed one message that jumped out at me. There was an inspection scheduled for mid-morning, but the welder hadn't completed their portion. *Shit,* I thought. If we had to reschedule the inspection, that would throw everything out of sync, including my time off. I knew I should have called True or William, but my intuition told me to do differently and head on over to the job site myself. Surely, I could get one of the contractors to help me really quick. Then, I would already be there to ensure the inspection passed.

I jumped up and put on my coat as Chelle came into the office.

"Girl, I gotta run over to the job site. There's a problem. I think I can fix it," I told Chelle as I zoomed by her. I didn't have time to answer any questions. I got in my car and headed over there. As I suspected, traffic was heavy. Had I stayed behind to talk to Chelle, I might have missed my window of opportunity.

I kept checking my watch. I was pressed for time, and this freaking traffic was nerve-wracking!

When I finally reached the job site, I walked around looking for Cathy the foreman to give me a full rundown of what exactly was needed to be ready for the inspection. I saw a plank that appeared to be out of place. I had the bright idea to fix it. I climbed the scaffolding grabbed the hammer that was lying next to the plank, and set it. *There that should do*, I thought. I saw the foreman on the other side of the building. I climbed down the scaffolding holding on tight, but once I got down to the last few stairs, my foot slipped, causing me to hit the ground. I opened my eyes to people screaming.

"Chance, say something. Can you hear me?" Cathy the foreman yelled.

I shook my head and tried to sit up.

"Don't move," she said. "The paramedics are on their way."

I thought about True and how he told me not to come on the job site about a month ago once I really started showing. I had to get up. I couldn't let him find out I was here. "I'm okay," I lied. I pulled myself up. "Let me call my doctor. I'm sure she'll fit me in," I stressed.

My back hurt like hell, but I limped to the car anyway.

"Chance, at least let me call your husband," the foreman begged, following me to my car.

"Thank you so much, but I'll take care of everything," I said before closing my car door.

I figured if I laid down a while, I would be okay. I was shaken up by the unexpected fall. I was so distraught as I moved into the intersection when a car came barreling through. I felt the car's impact jerking me like a ragdoll and its blaring horn before I blacked out. The next moments came in flashes - a man ripping the wires from the steering wheel to stop the blaring horn, me sitting in a field. But I was confused because I swore I could still see myself sitting in the car. The contractors and foreman from the job site ran over to the accident. The foreman waved the ambulance down.

"She's over here," she yelled.

The EMT's tried to open the car door, but it was stuck. Some of the contractors brought over tools to help pry my door open.

"I'm over here," I mouthed, but it was like I was invisible.

"Get the stretcher," someone yelled.

Beginning to feel chilled, I was weaker than I'd ever been before. I had a weird sensation that I was free. Seeing a woman in a car, I was curious about who she was. As I recognized myself, it felt like a giant magnet was pulling me. I wasn't frightened. I looked prettier and younger than I remembered. It was weird seeing myself as three dimensional. I was enjoying this new weightless pain-free body. I wanted to follow the pull that was calling me but instead, my attention went back to the woman.

I watched as they pulled my limp body out of the car, and then they rushed me into the ambulance and climbed in with me. They did CPR on me as I watched. When all of a sudden, I felt like I was back in my body. Immediately noticing the cumbersome weight, pain and sickness I wanted to go back.

"We got a pulse," I heard one of them say.

"Ma'am, what is your name? Are you pregnant?" One of them asked.

"No," I answered.

"She's confused. Let's get her to the hospital STAT," the other EMT said.

I remember being rushed into a CT scan right before an officer asked to take photos of my injures. I heard the doctors whispering that my contractions weren't slowing down.

Chapter Ten

TRUE

I had just finished my morning reports and was ready to go out in the field. I looked down at my buzzing phone and recognized the number.

"Hey, Cathy, good morning," I greeted. She was the foreman on our residential projects. Chance must have directed her my way.

"True, your wife was here this morning. She fell off a scaffolding and then left here in a rush and got into a car accident. It's bad. They're taking Chance to Mt. Carmel."

I had tunnel vision after that. I had to get to my wife and baby.

"William, hold things down. Chance was in an accident," I yelled on the way out the door. I drove as fast as I could while still trying to be safe on the slick roads. Hell, it wouldn't do us any good if both of us were in accidents. That woman of mine was so damn hardheaded. What was she doing on a damn scaffolding? I beat on the steering wheel at the thought of her falling and then getting into an accident.

I picked up my cell phone and hit the button to dial Chance's mother before hitting the hands-free button.

"Hello, True. Is the baby coming early?" Mom asked before I could speak.

"Chance's been in an accident. Meet me at Mt. Carmel. I don't have any details. I'll send a car. I don't want you driving," I instructed before hanging up.

I pulled into the emergency room parking lot and rushed into the hospital.

"My wife, Chance Fourlove, was brought in by an ambulance. She was in an accident."

I couldn't get the words out fast enough. I had to see my wife. I had to lay eyes on her and know she was going to make it and find out if our baby survived the wreck. I was almost weak at the knees, thinking about the trauma. I was mad at her for being so hardheaded, but the fear that consumed my heart was greater.

"Sir, she's been taken back for a CT scan. We will come get you as soon as they get her into a room," the receptionist told me.

"Can you give me any details?" I asked. The woman shook her head no before speaking.

"I'm sorry that information is confidential and not given to me."

I turned my back to the woman and walked into the waiting room. I picked up my cell phone to order the Uber for my mother-in-law, who was probably dressed and ready to go. I texted her:

"Mom, the Uber will be there in ten minutes. They have not let me back to see Chance yet," I hit the send button.

It was plain torture not knowing what was going on back there. I wanted to scream at the top of my lungs.

"Mr. Fourlove, you can come on back," a nurse directed. "The doctor will bring you up to date."

We walked fast, which scared me.

"Mr. Fourlove?" The doctor greeted after we passed the double doors.

"Yes," I answered, reaching out to shake his hand.

"Your wife is okay on the surface. She was a little confused and scared. We gave her a mild sedative to help her relax. We also had to give her something to help stop the contractions, which we're still monitoring. We don't want her to deliver the baby today unless we feel either her or the baby is under duress. We will keep her because we need to run some more tests. And as I said, if we're unable to get the contractions under control, we might be delivering a baby," the doctor told me.

"So, they are both alive and well?" I wanted confirmation.

"Yes, like I said on the surface, everything is okay. We need to make sure there is no internal damage, so we took the CT scan. We did get the baby's heartbeat, and mother and baby are being monitored. We're not out of the woods yet, but the prognosis is good." The doctor put his hand on my shoulder as reassurance.

I walked into the room. It looked like a trauma center with all kinds of monitors and people running in and out. I heard the baby's familiar heartbeat that I was used to hearing when we went in for doctors' appointments.

"Chance, baby, how are you feeling?" I questioned, giving my beautiful wife a soft kiss on her forehead, not wanting to hurt her. She didn't answer, but she looked at me with tear-filled eyes. The look Chance gave almost broke me down. I instantly remembered the feeling I had when I lost my parents years ago. It was the greatest pain I'd ever known.

I grabbed her hand and kissed it.

"Aaaaaaggggg!" She cried out in agony.

"What's wrong, baby?" I asked as a nurse whisked by me.

"She's having a contraction. Breathe, Chance," the nurse told her. "Take a deep breath and try to relax. We don't want you to have this baby yet if we can help it."

I thumbed her hand in an attempt to console her.

"Chance," my mother in law called out, which seemed to upset Chance all over again. Mom gave me a half hug, but it was Chance she needed to lay eyes on.

"Hi, baby," Mom whispered.

"Mom," Chance managed to mumble before the tears flowed again.

"Don't cry, baby. We got you. Just let me know what you need, and we're on it, love," mom told her.

Minutes later, Chance dozed off, and mom motioned for

me to follow her as we stepped into the hall.

"True, what did the doctor say?" She questioned.

"They're trying to stop her contractions."

"Oh my God, she's having contractions," mom repeated just as the doctor approached us.

"Mr. Fourlove," he said.

"Yes, and this is Chance's mother, Mrs. Wright," I introduced.

"Great, I get to speak to both of you." The doctor grabbed the clipboard from under his arm and flipped a few pages back.

"Okay, let's see. Chance Fourlove, yes, here it is. So, Chance has a severe case of whiplash and a bruised lung. The baby from what we can tell is okay," the doctor explained.

Mom and I seemed to sigh at the same time.

"Last I checked, the contractions have slowed from every two minutes to now 15 minutes apart, so I am hopeful we can turn this thing around. It would help if Chance healed from the whiplash and bruised lung before birthing a baby, which could be extremely painful. I gotta get going, but I will check back in a few to keep you updated on her contractions." The doctor stuck the clipboard back under his arm.

"Thank you," I told him.

"No problem," he answered before moving on to the next room.

"True, I need to go grab a sandwich and a bottle of water. I haven't had anything today. I need something on my stomach before taking this blood pressure medicine," Mom said, digging down into her purse to retrieve the little brown bottle.

"Would you bring me a coffee back?" I asked.

"I sure will, sugar."

I headed back into the room and pulled a chair up next to the bed. I sat elbows to knees with head in hands. *Thank you, God.* I said inside my head. *I know we're not entirely in the clear yet, but God, thank you for not taking my wife and baby from me. I don't think I could survive losing either one of them. But God, please heal my wife and baby of any unknown injuries.* I sniffed as the lone tear escaped my eye.

"True, I'm so sorry," I heard Chance say.

"Baby, don't worry about it. I'm just thankful the both of you are okay." I quickly swiped at the tear that escaped my eye. I had to man up and let my wife know I was here to get her through this thing. My emotions got the best of me, but I was feeling more confident the more time passed with no contractions.

Chapter Eleven

CHANCE

"It hurts to breathe," I said, taking shallow breaths.

"You have a bruised lung. I don't think they can do much for that. It has to heal with time. You also have whiplash," True explained.

"I feel like shit," was the best way to describe what I felt like. I grabbed my belly because I could feel my baby moving around. I couldn't lie. The whole time I was depressed about this pregnancy. Now, the life inside me had a whole different intensity. My motherly instinct must have kicked in because I would die first before I let anything happen to my baby. I just wished I felt that way this morning before I climbed that scaffolding. I tried to shake my head at the thought, but the stiff collar stopped me from making a move.

My mother walked back into the room. I couldn't turn my head, but I used my eyes to follow her. She carried a bottle of water and a cup of coffee. I could smell it. My senses had been heightened this whole pregnancy. I felt like a superhero because even leather smelled like a fresh piece of meat. I almost gagged at the thought. Mom pulled a chair up to the other side of my bed. She placed a hand on my belly.

"How's Nana's baby?" I could feel the baby moving around under her hand, which was enough to make me cry again.

"Now, Chance, I know your husband isn't going to say anything. And I don't want you to think I'm chastising you, but what on God's green earth were you doing on a scaffolding?"

I let out a long-winded sigh before cringing under the pain of my lung.

"Aaaggghh," I yelled out. "I'm sorry. I keep forgetting about the pain. Mom, I don't have a good explanation for you. I honestly wish I could take the whole day back," I cried.

"Like I said, I'm not trying to chastise you. I genuinely

wanted to know what was going on inside your head, especially when you have this strong ass husband of yours, not to mention a slew of other people you could have called on. Let me just say this one thing, and then I'm done with it. I understand you're in a male-dominated industry, but there are going to be times that, as a mother, you might need to stand back to protect your child." Mom grabbed my hands and squeezed them tight. "It's also a mother's duty to cuss her child out after she scares her half to death."

Tears flowed freely from my mother's eyes. She was right. I had been reckless in my moves this morning. This whole accident could have been avoided.

What if I'd killed my baby because I was too busy trying to be a boss? The thought of it all, shattered my heart to pieces. I could barely see through my tear-filled eyes. Mom must have noticed because she grabbed a Kleenex and wiped my face for me.

"How's everyone doing today?" Doctor Ghiloni asked, walking into my room.

"Pretty good," I heard my mother respond.

"So, here's the deal. We were able to stop the contrac-

tions. We're going to keep Chance another day for observation, and if all is well tomorrow, she can go home," she
stated, looking directly at me. "I don't want this baby here
for another two to three weeks if we can help it, only
because the baby is still pretty small. Another couple of
pounds will do the baby well. Baby's tend to gain around a
pound a week at this stage," the doctor stated.

"Sounds good," my husband said.

"But young lady, you will be on strict bed rest. You will
only be able to get up to use the restroom. You are not to do
any housework, lifting, or even stairs. You got that?" Doc
asked.

"Yes, thanks," I replied, cringing through the pain once
again.

"I'll be back tomorrow to check on you and see if we
can discharge you. In the meantime, try to get some rest so
your body can heal."

"Thank you," my mother called out as the doctor left
the room.

"I think I will take the doctor up on that nap now," I
commented.

"True, why don't you go on and take care of the business

with Chances' car and wrap up your business at the office. We can take shifts. I'll be ready to go home when you get back," mom told him.

"Yeah, let me see if I can track the vehicle down. It was probably towed. I might need to call Triple-A." True looked at his watch, then he bent down to kiss me.

"I love you, babe. I'll be right back," he crooned before grabbing his coat and leaving the room.

Chapter Twelve

TRUE

I stopped at the nurse's station to see if they had any information on my wife's car. Hell, I didn't even know where the accident was.

"Hello, my wife in room 204 was in a car accident this morning. I was wondering if you had any information on where the accident was so I can get her car," I asked, thinking I sounded totally crazy.

"Oh, yes, there was an officer here taking photos of your wife's injuries this morning. He left this card."

"Great. That's exactly what I need," I told the nice woman behind the desk. I headed out into the long-empty corridor to make some phone calls. Leaning against the wall, I dialed the detective's phone number.

"Detective Stoaks," he answered. By the grace of God, he

answered the phone, which surprised me on a Friday afternoon.

"Good afternoon, Detective. My name is True Fourlove. My wife Chance was in a car accident this morning. I'm trying to track down her vehicle," I told him.

"Oh, yes. Some people moved her car out of the intersection over on Grammercy and Easton Way. It was moved onto the lot of the construction site there, so we didn't tow the vehicle. How is your wife doing, by the way?" He asked.

"She's banged up pretty bad and still under observation, but we're thankful she's alive. Do you know what happened or who was at fault?" I questioned the detective.

"Apparently, an elderly gentleman drove the other car. We're not sure if he was under medical duress, which may have caused him to run the light because he was pretty confused. You can go online and get a copy of the police report. You'll probably need to contact your insurance company," Detective Stoaks advised me.

"Thanks for all your assistance," I said. "Have a good day."

"You too," he noted.

Next, I dialed William's number. "How is she?" He blurted out immediately.

"Awe, man, she's banged up pretty bad, but they are alive," I ran my hand down my face trying to hold back the sudden rush of emotions. "Hey, I need a favor, man?" "What's up," Will responded.

"I need you to ride over to the construction site with me to see what the damage is to Chance's car. I'll swing by and get you."

"Bet," I heard William say. By this time, I made it to the emergency room double doors and headed to my car. I hopped in. It was cold out, but the adrenaline that coursed through my veins wouldn't allow me to worry about the frigid temperatures. I was only about ten minutes away from the job when I pulled up. I noticed William watching for me. He took off in a slow jog towards my Lincoln, which was now nice and warm.

"Thanks for helping me out, bro," I said.

"You know it's no problem. So, what exactly happened? I didn't call because I knew you would be busy," Will replied.

"Man, first she went to a job site this morning and fell

coming down the scaffolding. I guess she was almost at the bottom but still fell. Then I guess she was spooked and jumped in the car, where an elderly gentleman ran the light and hit her. Chance was having labor pains, which they were finally able to stop, and she has a bruised lung and whiplash."

"Oh my God, what the hell was she doing on a scaffolding?" Will looked my way in angst.

"You know she's hardheaded," I blew out air.

"Damn," Will said.

"Tell me about it."

I pulled into the job site next to Chance's car. She'd been hit on the driver's side.

"The car is fucked up," I huffed.

"It can be fixed," William reminded me.

"I know. It just hurts. I could have lost my family," I held back hot tears. It was the sight of the vehicle that made it a reality of the pain she'd gone through. William got out of the car and started cleaning out Chance's glovebox. I called Triple-A to have the vehicle towed to a body shop.

"I got everything of value out of there," William said.

I held a finger up to him to motion that I was on the

phone.

"Thanks," I said to the insurance agent on the phone.

"Thanks, man. I think everything I need to do concerning the accident has been taken care of," I explained once I finished the phone call.

Noticing Cathy, the foreman on the job site approaching the car, I rolled down my window.

"Hey, True... William," Cathy nodded at us. "How's Chance? I've been a nervous wreck all day."

"Pretty beat up, but she and the baby are okay."

"Thank goodness," she replied. "You know I wouldn't have let her get up there. I didn't even know she was here until I saw her lying on the ground."

"I don't blame you. My wife is hardheaded," I laughed and shook my head at the same time.

"Well, you two try to have a good weekend," she said, backing away from the car.

"You too," I responded, and William waved.

"Man, you know whatever you need, I got you. I can hold down the office if you need to stay with Chance or whatever," William told me.

"I know you do. I appreciate you. Do you mind if I stop

by Chance's job? I need to let them know what's going on," I asked.

"I'm along for the ride," he responded.

In my mind, I was ready to get back to Chance. I was thankful to have taken care of all the business at hand. The bricks were slowly falling off my shoulders one by one. Each one was allowing me to breathe a little easier even though we weren't out of the woods yet, we were a little closer.

I pulled up to the One-Stop-Shop Design House where Chance worked, and William and I went inside. After telling them the long story of the day's events, everyone was visibly shaken.

"Can we go to the hospital?" Chelle asked.

"She's under observation in the neonatal center, and they only allow two family members to visit. If all goes well, she will be discharged tomorrow. Once she's settled, you can come by the house to see her. Right now, she needs to rest so we can give her injuries some time to heal before she delivers the baby. But I will definitely keep everyone posted. Chelle, you're in charge," I said.

I handed Zen my business card. "Here's my number in

case you need me for any reason,"

"Thanks, man," we fist-bumped.

"William will be running things at our office. We'll have to all pull together to get through this tough time. Luckily, this is our slow season so, I don't expect we'll have anything out of the ordinary. We should pretty much take the orders and plan for the springtime rush," I explained.

"Sounds good," Chelle and everyone chimed in.

"Great, well, let me get back to my wife and baby. I'll let her know everyone sends prayers and healing," I told them.

William and I got back in the car so that I could drop him off at work. The evening was approaching, and the rush hour traffic was building. I pulled up to our building, and William hopped out.

"Thanks again," I said.

"No problem, keep me posted."

"I will," I answered, before backing out of the spot. I was thankful to have William. He was my brother, and even though we weren't brothers by blood, our bond made us that way. This all made me realize that family was necessary.

Chapter Thirteen

CHANCE

I opened my eyes, trying to remember where I was. The monitors and machines hooked up to me and my baby reminded me that I didn't just have a bad dream, that this was my reality. My man walked into the room. He moved differently. His swagger was more pronounced. And I wondered why his sexy ass dimples always rendered me speechless. Not long after he hit the corner, the room held a tantalizing scent. That scent I would never tire of.

"Hey Mom, hey Babe," True said, bending down to give me sugar.

"Hey, True," mom answered. "Did you get the business with the car taken care of?"

"I sure did. It went better than I expected. I spoke with the detective and found out it was an elderly gentleman who hit Chance. They think he might have had something medical-related that may have confused him while driving," True explained.

"Oh, my goodness, I pray he's okay!" Mom stated.

"Me too," I groaned, remembering my pains instantly.

"How are you feeling baby? Do you need anything?" Mom asked.

"I want to sit up a little," I told her. Mom reached over and grabbed the controller to the bed and sat me up. "Mmm," I moaned quietly. "Thanks, mom. Babe, can you get me some ice chips?" I asked my husband.

"Sure," he answered, grabbing the pitcher they had sitting on the bedside tray. A nurse walked into my room with a tray of food.

"Hello," she sang. "Do you feel like eating a little something?"

"I can try," I answered. I watched the nurse put the tray on the bedside table and roll it closer to me.

"It's soup and crackers, along with some jello. Just ring the bell if you need anything else," the lovely nurse told me. I liked her. She didn't seem like she hated her job like some of the other nurses I had run in's with. I understood it was a hard job. You had to have the right kind of mindset to care for people.

Mom lifted the cover off the soup and laid the napkin in my lap.

"Thanks, mom, I can get it from here," I commented.

I was hit on the left side of my body, so I was lucky to be right-handed. True came back with my ice chips and poured them into a Styrofoam cup, placing them close to me.

"What did they give you, soup?" He asked, answering his own question.

"Yes," I also answered. I picked up the plastic soup spoon and dipped up some soup. The warmth of it felt good going down my dry throat. I guess I was hungry.

"Well, now that you're all settled, I'm going to get on back home. But I will be back bright and early. You know I don't like to stay out too late," mom added.

"I know. I thank you so much for spending the day up here with me."

"Girl, you don't have to thank me. True, did you order me a ride?" Mom asked him.

"I'm doing it now. The Uber will be here in five minutes,

mom," True answered.

"They're fast. Let me get my coat."

True got up and helped mom into her coat. Mom kissed me on the forehead.

"I'll call you later, Chance," mom noted.

"Come on, mom," True stated. "Let me walk you down and make sure you get to your car."

"I'll be right back, babe," he told me.

I tried to nod my head, glad they took the plastic brace off my neck and replaced it with a softer, more pliable version. I sat there and continued to eat my soup and crackers. Thinking about my day and how blessed I was to be alive at this moment. Moments later, True came back. He sat closer to the bed where mom had been sitting. He rubbed my leg.

"I'm so glad to see you up and eating," he pointed out.

"I know, me, too. Are you mad at me?" I asked, noticing he hadn't said much to me today.

"No, I'm not. I can't lie though. I was glad your mom got on your tail because Lord knows I wanted to!" He laughed.

I smiled, trying to suppress the giggle I knew would cause me pain.

"You enjoyed that, hun? Watching me get cussed out by my mom." I smiled brightly now. I couldn't fight the giggles. I laughed and groaned all at the same time.

"You are so goofy," my husband joked.

Once I finished my food, the nurses who seemed to come in every hour on the hour returned to take my vitals, wanted to do a pelvic check. They had to lay the bed back down, which did not feel good at all.

"Okay, everything feels fine with the cervix," the nurse stated, pulling the rubber gloves off her hands and covering me back up. "Can I get you anything?" She asked.

"No, I'm fine," I answered, pushing the remote's button to sit back up. The nurse pulled the curtain back before going out the door.

"I hope they let you out of here tomorrow," True urged.

"You and me both. They tell you to rest but messing with you every few minutes," I laughed.

"I think it's time you and I decide what we're going to name the baby. Especially since I almost went into labor today," I noted.

True rubbed his hand down his face and lifted his eyebrows.

"Yeah, you're right. So, what do you have in mind?" He asked.

It was an excellent way to pass the time, but after a while of throwing out a series of names, I didn't think we were any closer to the answer.

"I don't know, babe," I said. "I think it's because I don't know what we're having."

"Yeah," he answered. "It feels so random."

True picked up the remote. I could tell he was tired, and so was I. He flipped through the channels before saying, "I haven't eaten a thing all day. Let me run down to the café and grab a bite."

"Okay," I mumbled before dozing off.

Chapter Fourteen

TRUE

I headed down to the café to grab a bite. I sat down at a table alone, trying to give myself a minute to wind down. I picked up my phone and scrolled Facebook. It was boring, as usual. I dialed my homies number.

"Yoo," I said when he picked up.

"What up, bro?" Will asked.

"Shit," I answered. "Told you I'd let you know how's she's doing."

"Cool."

"Yeah, she's coming around. She ate a little soup. That seemed to perk her up," I explained.

"That's great," I heard Steal in the background asking how she was. "She's cool," William told her.

"Okay, man, I'll get with you tomorrow," I said.

"Bet," William answered. I finished up my sandwich and headed back to the room, where I promptly fell asleep.

Chance's mom was at the hospital bright and early like she said she would be.

"I drove today, True. The roads aren't that bad," mom told me.

"Good morning, sweetie. I wanted to be here when the doctor came just in case I had any questions," mom added.

"I'm going down for coffee." I noted.

"Get us all some," Chance chimed in.

"I will." I was glad to step out of the room and catch a breather. Hospitals really weren't my thing. This whole ordeal reminded me of my parents being killed in a car accident years ago. It was something I intentionally put out of my mind. Knowing I could have lost my wife and unborn baby the same way triggered those memories that plagued my mind.

"Three coffees, please, one decaf," I told the line worker. I pulled money from my wallet and paid the cashier. I added sugar packets and cream to the empty spot on the drink carrier and headed back to the room. The doctor was in the room talking with Chance when I walked in.

"Good morning, Doctor Ghiloni," I said. Doctor Ghiloni was Chance's regular OB.

"Good morning, True. I was just telling your wife and mother in law that I would go ahead and sign the release papers today. Chance seems stable enough to go home and rest in her own bed," she announced.

"That's good news," I said, placing the coffee down on the bedside table.

"Chance, you have my number. Please call me if anything changes," Doctor Ghiloni told her before leaving the room.

"Yes," I exclaimed.

"Let's get you dressed," Mom said. "True, you can get the car warmed up, and we'll meet you in front. The nurse will bring her down in a wheelchair," mom instructed.

"I'm on it," I grabbed my coffee and took a nice long, much-needed swig," I hit the but to start my car from the hospital and headed that way. I grabbed the scraper out the back and got the windows cleaned off. I pulled up to the hospital patient's loading area and waited on them to come out. When I saw them approaching the doors, I hopped out, and opened the car door, helped my wife into the vehicle, and told my mother in law to get in so I could take her to her car.

"Thanks," I told the nurse.

"True, I'm going to stop by the store, and then I'll be by the house," mom said.

"Okay," I answered as mom jumped out to get inside her car. I put my hand in my wife's lap as I drove, careful not to hit any bumps too hard or make any sudden moves.

When we got home, I pulled into our driveway and opened the garage door. I jumped out, picked Chance up, carried her into the house, and sat her on the couch.

"Wait here," I instructed. I wasn't taking any chances with Mrs. Hardheaded. She couldn't be trusted. After I ran back outside, I pulled the car into the garage. Once back in the house, I helped my wife out of her coat. Then I picked her up and carried her upstairs to our room.

"You let me know if you need anything. Doc said you could walk to the bathroom, but that's it. Don't let me find out you doing anything else," I joked but not really.

"I know. I learned my lesson," Chance admitted.

I took her into the restroom and started the shower after taking my coat off, allowing it to drop to the floor. Slowly undressing my baby, I helped her step into the hot water. Then I took my clothes off and stepped in behind her. Grasping the soap and washcloth, I gently scrubbed her down. I was taking precautions to be extremely gentle with her back and neck area. I looked up, and tears were falling from her eyes. Placing my mouth over hers, I planted kisses that were slow and thoughtful. I was going to give her what she needed, mind, body, and soul. My gaze dropped from her eyes to her shoulders and then to her breasts. A soft moan escaped her lips as my tongue caressed her sensitive, swollen nipples.

"Damn baby," I swore out loud. Best believe she had my manhood rising to the occasion as it involuntarily throbbed against her body. I knew we couldn't risk having sex. I just wanted to make her feel good. So much pain had been inflicted on her over the years.

"I want you so bad, right now. Please," Chance begged.

I turned off the water. I stepped out of the shower and wrapped a towel around my waist. Then I wrapped one around my wife and carried her to our room, placing her softly across the bed.

"Please, True," she whined again.

I stuck two fingers inside. "Oh my God, you're so wet,"

I whispered. I didn't want to hurt her, hell. She'd just gotten out of the hospital. She gasped in sweet agony as I took a taste. My tongue lapped the warm honey, and it wasn't long before she exploded a downpour.

"Ooooooo," she cooed as I slid my tip-in, and the gush she released was enough to bring me to a crest almost immediately.

"Ohhh Shiii," I growled. I wanted to lay down and fall asleep with her in my arms. But I knew my mother in law was probably on her way. I threw on some gray sweats and grabbed a warm washcloth to wash Chance.

"Um, baby."

"Yeah, I answered."

"That was the best I've felt in forever," she swooned. "But you know mom is coming over, and you can't freestyle in those gray jogging pants," she giggled.

I shook my head. "You're right. Let me put some drawls on. I can't be fighting you and your mama off," I laughed.

"Boy, stop," she laughed.

I put a pair of white cotton bikini panty's on Chance and an oversized t-shirt. I carefully placed the collar back on her neck and carried her downstairs to the theatre room.

I put her on the chaise lounge with a comforter. By this time, the doorbell was ringing. I let Mom in and helped her with her bags.

"Make yourself at home were in here watching TV," I told her.

"Go on, I'm going to whip up a few meals for you guys to have this week," she said.

"Thanks, that sounds good," I gave her a peck on the cheek and headed back to the family room where I could finally rest my eyes in peace.

Chapter Fifteen

CHANCE

Damn, it was good to be back home. I still had chills traveling down my spine from my husband's sweet sensations he'd just laid on me. It was like the pain I felt from the accident intensified my pleasure. True climbed under the comforter with me as our legs intertwined. I swear it was only minutes before I heard his soft snores. I found a good movie and watched it until I could no longer hold my eyes open.

About an hour later, mom woke us for an early dinner. She moved a couple of modern TV trays up to the couch and placed our plates and beverages on them before grabbing her own. True handed me my plate since we were on the chaise lounge.

There was another Christmas moving coming on, and it was a relaxing lazy day at home with my mom and my man. I couldn't have been happier considering everything that happened.

It was the next day, Chelle and Trinity came by to sit with me while True went to shoot some basketball with William. I knew he was ready to burn off a little steam. I welcomed the break as well.

"What's up?" Chelle and Trinity sang as they came through the door.

"I'll be back in a couple of hours, babe," True kissed my cheek on his way out the door. I was sitting in the living room today. The girls took their coats off and laid them across the armchair by the door. Trinity laid a couple of big books on the coffee table.

"How are you feeling, honey?" Trinity asked, giving me air kisses before sitting down.

"I'm still a little stiff but much better today," I responded.

"Girl, we're so thankful you and the baby are alright," Chelle added.

"I know it was dumb. I don't know what got into me." I looked down in embarrassment.

"You ain't used to waiting around on people to do stuff for you," Trinity said.

"I know," I agreed.

"Anyway, I know you're tired of talking about it. Let's look at these wedding books. I need you guys to help me plan," Trinity squealed.

"Chelle, go into the kitchen. There should be a pen and pad on the counter," I instructed.

"Okay." Chelle headed into the kitchen. "Chance, I'm going to get us a snack while I'm in there, too," she said.

"Go ahead," I told her.

"So, Trinity, what type of wedding do you want to have, church, destination, backyard?" I questioned. By this time, Chelle came back in with a bowl of chips, cups and a pitcher of lemonade.

"That's a good question?" She responded.

"When do you plan on getting married? Do you want something large or more intimate?" Chelle asked.

"Geesh, so many questions to answer," Trinity grabbed her head. "Hell, I lightweight want to go to the justice of the peace and call it a day," she joked.

Trinity grabbed a handful of chips. "What do two people who have been married before care about a wedding?" She asked.

"Have you asked O' his thoughts?" I asked.

"Yeah, he doesn't care as long as I'm happy. I think my fear is I've kind of been at odds with my family. You know?" Trinity asked.

"It's going to be your party. You get to be in charge of who comes or not," Chelle noted.

"Yeah, you're right," Trinity agreed.

"Chelle, write down intimate," I suggested.

"Okay," Chelle said.

"What about your colors?" I asked.

"Let me think about it for a minute." She picked up one of the wedding books and started flipping through it. "I like this teal and white ombre trumpet style dress. And to set it off, I want my bridesmaids to have these rust-colored dresses. They have three different styles, so each of you can pick your style," Trinity informed us.

"Let me see. Hold the book up," I said. "Oh my gosh, yes, that's beautiful," I commented.

"And different," Chelle agreed. "Those colors together are fire."

"Thanks, but why does planning a wedding have to be so stressful?" Trinity whined.

"I don't know," Chelle pondered.

"Have you had any more problems with O's ex-wife showing up at the salon?" I asked.

"Girl no, ain't nobody got time for that," Trinity snapped her fingers.

"Let me find out, Trin. I got your back. That girl better get her life!" Chelle was pumped because her head rolled and lips smacked. She was so animated.

"Right, I got you, girl," I chimed in with my neck brace on.

"If you don't sit your ass down somewhere," Trinity said, and we all cracked up.

Nah, but seriously though ya'll I'm feeling Zen. He's so damn fine. I love a man with big strong arms cause I ain't no little chic. I need someone that can swoop a sistah up because I like a man to pin me up against that wall, and you know." By this time, Chelle was up and doing some kind of snake move with her body. I couldn't shake my head, but it was hilarious.

"I just don't think I could be with someone romantically that I work with because I go to work to get away. I don't need to see his ass all day," Chelle laughed.

"If I could high five you right now, I would. Things have gotten much stronger between True and I since we aren't in each other's face all day," I chimed in.

"I feel you," Trinity added. "Oh, wait, I forgot. 'O' and I work together, kind of. I ain't going to lie. We have slipped away for a quickie," she said with a sneaky grin.

"Okay, okay, I might be feeling that then," Chelle said. I loved the way she bounced when she talked.

"Uh, no," I added.

"I forgot you're an old married woman now," Chelle laughed.

I rolled my eyes at her since I couldn't roll my whole neck. "I got 210 pounds of solid man that likes this old woman," I joked.

"Go, girl," Chelle laughed.

We had a good time this afternoon planning Trinity's

wedding and joking around it helped me to not wallow in my pain. I loved my girls.

Chapter Sixteen

TRUE

I met up with the fellas to play some ball. I was ready to blow off a little steam. I was killing them with my impromptu three-pointers.

"Damn, son. Why you out here showboating like you still in college or something," Kelvin joked.

"I let him have that because bro had a rough week," Will chimed in.

"Nah, you know this is how I always roll," I bragged.

"Whatever," William sneered.

After we ran the ball a few more times, we sat down against the wall to take a break.

"What are ya'll getting into this evening?" I asked.

"Man, we're actually meeting up with Steals' parents who are in town for a holiday dinner. We're doing it early because her parents are going on a cruise for Christmas," William said.

"Okay, sounds cool," I told him.

"Yeah, Brian and I are going to the movie later and maybe stop by his sister's house to play some spades," said Kelvin.

I nodded my head. "Word. Tell your sister I said what's up," I commented. Kelvin was another childhood friend of mine. I didn't know he liked boys until we were in college. I always felt he was kind of different, but he was still cool as hell. I never treated him any differently than any other of my friends. Hell, he did all the same stuff I liked to do - play ball, shoot pool and was competitive like me, so he's always been a part of the crew.

"I will," Kelvin answered. "She's still crazy as hell," he laughed.

"Your sister is off the hook," William chimed in.

"Well, Chance and I will be chilling at the crib since she's on bed rest," I reminded them.

"It'll be over soon, and you'll be wishing you had some chill time," William laughed.

"I know, everyone has been telling us the same thing," I

said. "So, Will, how's the married life been treating you?" I smirked.

"Man, I'm loving it so far. Me and Steal be kicking it on the real," William said, the side of his mouth quirked upward. I laughed. "Too good for words, hun?"

"Boy, you're sprung," Kelvin laughed, too. I had to admit I was thankful he'd found his own woman to love. We hadn't seen William like this over someone in forever. Well, actually, I had seen him like this, over Chance. But it had always been the elephant in the room. They'd always denied it, but I wasn't dumb. I know what I'd seen in their faces was way more than admiration. Hell, at one point and time, I didn't even care because I was on the chase my damn self. I groaned inwardly at the twinge of disappointment I felt. I remembered it like it was yesterday. I planned to fix William up with someone because I thought he and Chance were getting too close for comfort. Chance wasn't my wife back then, but love could be a powerful drug. I knew love could make a blind man see. The crazy thing about it was I hadn't allowed myself to love, not really love someone. I thought love was having a fine piece on my arm. I thought love was something I could show up for when I felt like it. I didn't understand the commitment of it being like a full-time job. It wasn't until I thought I had a child with Lace and that little boy Grayson pulled at my heart-strings. I would have gone to the end of the earth for that little boy and back. And then it was ripped away from me. The anguish I'd suffered before realizing the light at the end of the tunnel was my wife.

God had used me as an example many times, each time allowing me to step up. And each time, me failing to realize love was right in front of me. I truly believed I understood when I thought my life would be ripped away from me once again. When I'd heard my wife had fallen and was then in a car accident. The lump that filled my throat almost took my air and swiped my feet from under me. It was almost too much to bear.

"True," I heard William say.

"Yeah," I tried to play off the fact I'd been deep in thought and didn't know how much of the conversation I'd missed.

"Bro, I said I was going to get out of here. I have stuff to do," William repeated.

"Yeah, me, too," Kelvin agreed.

"I guess I do need to make sure my girl is alright," I said, standing up. We all fist-bumped before putting on our jackets, gathering our things, and heading to our cars.

I got in my car sitting there for a moment, giving it a second to heat up. I needed that time to play ball because the running, the exercise cleared my mind, giving me the insight on my relationship, on my life that I needed. I was becoming that grown man I always desired to be. I felt it in the depths of my soul.

I pulled out of the parking lot and headed home. I called my wife using the hands-free setting in my car. "Hey, babe. I'm going to stop by the store. I'm calling to see if you need anything," I said when she answered.

"Nah, I'm good. I'll see you when you get here," Chance replied.

I pulled into the store parking lot. I always parked far away from the store because these folks would let their carts hit your car. They didn't care, but it pissed me off. And no matter how far away I parked, it was always someone next to me when I came out. I scoffed at the thought. I needed two things, flowers for my baby and two pints of our favorite ice-cream. I had a date with my wife. I paid for my items and drove home. I pulled into the garage and headed inside.

"I'm home," I called out.

"In here," she said. I put the ice cream in the freezer and headed into the living room with the huge bouquet behind my back.

"Hey brother," Trinity said. I liked that about her. She always called me her brother. I was learning family was the people in our circle.

"Hey, sis," I answered. "What's up knucklehead, I mean Chelle," I joked.

She laughed. "Oh, you have jokes today," she smiled.

"Hi babe, how was the game," Chance asked.

I smacked my lips. "You know I whooped their asses," I declared. I whipped the flowers around, and Chance lit up.

"Awe," I heard them all coo.

"Thanks, True, they're beautiful," my wife said.

"Let me go put them in some water," I told her, pivoting on my feet.

"Don't forget to add the packet of plant food. They'll last longer," Chance reminded me.

I headed into the kitchen while they cackled about Lord

only knows what. I did what she told me. I even learned to clip the stems. I placed the assortment of flowers into the vase and took it back into the living room, where I placed it on the table.

"I love the colors in the arrangement," Trinity commented.

"Me, too," Chance agreed.

"Well, ladies, I've had enough wedding planning for the day," Chelle noted.

"Yeah," Trinity packed the books up.

"I'm so glad you guys came by to see me," Chance acknowledged.

"Yeah, and keep your behind off those scaffoldings," Chelle joked.

I twisted my face in disgust. It was true, though.

"I was just playing. Don't get all in your feelings," Chelle clarified.

"I know, girl," said Chance.

I helped the ladies with their coats and carried the big books out to Trinity's car. I was ready to get my evening of relaxation started. I took off in a slow jog towards the house to get out of the cold. I was huffing when I got back in the house, shutting the door behind me.

"Brrrrr, it's cold out there," I shivered.

"Baby, I need to go to the bathroom," she told me. I helped her up and guided her to the half bath.

"Let's watch a movie tonight," I proposed while waiting on her to come out.

"Sounds good." I heard the water running before the door opened. I helped my wife to the theatre room where she could sit on the chaise lounge and put her feet up. She laid down.

"I'm going to go shower and get in something comfortable," I noted.

"I'll be here; it's not like I can go anywhere." Chance sounded so pitiful. I bent down and grazed her forehead with my lips.

"Eeew, you stink boy."

Chapter Seventeen

CHANCE

I woke up to a hot plate of food. It smelled delicious. I hadn't had much of an appetite since the accident, but I knew I needed to fatten my little baby up. True helped me sit up, and I pulled my collar off.

"I can't stand this thing. I'm over it," I said, flinging it to the floor.

"Be careful," True advised. I propped myself up on the chaise lounge, and he placed the tray of food on my lap before he sat down next to me. Football was playing on the TV, which is probably why I'd fallen asleep so fast. I was so proud of my baby heating up my mother's casseroles for us to eat during the week.

"This is good," I noted. I loved my mom's cooking, and True did, too. I think it reminded him of his own mother's cooking.

"Who all showed up to play ball?" I asked.

"It was just me, William and Kelvin," True stated in between bites.

"Oh, okay, how's everyone doing?"

"William said Steal's family was having their Christmas dinner tonight because her parents were going on a cruise for the holidays."

"That sounds like so much fun," I envied.

"I know, right, and Kelvin and Brian were going to a movie and then over his crazy ass sisters' house to play some spades later," he laughed.

I raised my eyebrows. "Is she really that crazy?" I questioned.

"Hell yeah, she's always been that way since I've known her." he laughed. "I think she was born that way."

"Oh, my goodness," I blew out air before laughing. True picked up my tray and took it to the kitchen. Then he came back with two pints of ice cream and spoons.

"Since we can't drink wine, let's have an ice cream date. Cheers," he held his pint up, and I toasted it with mine.

"Cheers to you, babe, for giving me a chance," he told me.

"Awe, baby," I cooed. "You're so sweet."

"Nah, I mean it. You've been nothing but gracious in loving me," True smiled. His dimples appeared as if two fingers had squeezed his cheeks. I was uncomfortable with the fact that he was opening up to me. For so long, True had remained a mystery. He moved that way. Game face always on.

I dug my spoon into the cookies and cream ice cream and stuck it in my mouth. I was glad to use the ice cream as an escape from the words True spoke to me. Sometimes I couldn't help but think about how I almost lost him once again when he thought he had a baby with Lace. Was he only here for my baby, and I was just apart of the deal, I wondered? I wanted to ask him, but I also wanted to avoid any tension and conflict at this time. I was trying to remain calm for the sake of my pregnancy.

"Baby, why do I get the impression you've checked out on me," True asked.

"I'm sorry, True, but sometimes I wonder why you're even here?" I sat the ice cream down in the built-in cup holder on the couch and sighed.

"What do you mean?"

I tried to swallow my old fears and uncertainties. "Anytime another female flaunts her fat ass or baby in your face, you ghost me." I had a much stronger guard up now. I looked his way as a muscle flicked angrily in his jaw.

"You're right," he said, placing his ice cream in the cup holder also. "When Lace showed up on the scene, and I thought that was my baby, I immediately went into father mode. I wanted to love and protect that little boy. I admit I was torn at first. It felt good going over there playing house. But I saw the pain in your eyes. I also noticed you leaning on William for support," True stressed.

"What was I supposed to do?" I asked.

"I don't blame you. I haven't been a good guy. I haven't been the best example of a boyfriend, fiancé, or husband for that matter. Yet, you're always here putting up with my shit. It's time I lay it all out on the table because we never really talked about what happened with Lace and the baby because right after that, we found out you were pregnant. But I get it. We can't keep acting like it didn't happen," True swiped his face.

"I agree," I told him. "So, what happened with you and Lace?" I questioned.

True inhaled deeply before speaking. "A few times after going over there to see the baby, she hit on me. She would walk around half-naked, breastfeeding the baby in my face and shit. One day she even started to unbuckle my pants, but I stopped her. Now that I think about it, she was trying to get me in bed, probably hoping to get pregnant again."

I gave a choked laugh. "That bitch," I spewed. I looked at True. Detecting condescension in his attitude.

"But I also have a question for you. What were you going to do if Grayson was my baby? Were you going to leave me for William? Don't think I didn't notice he went on vacation because he was heartbroken over you."

"What do you think," I shot back.

True chuckled nastily.

"I'll tell you what I think. I think you being pregnant by me put a boomerang in your plans," True admitted.

"Don't try to put your shit off on me. Granted, William is a different kind of man than you are. And it has crossed my mind at times I wished you were more like him in the fact that he doesn't jump because any random throws a piece of ass at him. William was looking to connect with someone on a deeper level. He didn't like that you kept messing me over. I do think we admired each other at one point, but his integrity would have never allowed him to cross you as a friend," I explained.

"What about your integrity?" He asked.

"I'm still here, aren't I?" There was a long silence between us. He wanted a clean-cut answer, but I honestly couldn't give it to him. He picked up the melting ice cream containers and took them back to the kitchen. How did we even get here? I thought everything was going so well? And I had to ruin things.

True came back into the room and sat down next to me. He picked up my hand and interlocked our fingers.

"We're together for a reason. It's no mistake that you and I were drawn to each other. Today, I had a revelation that my commitment problems stem from me not having a real family for so long. I'm growing up, Chance. My mind is catching up with this body. I love you," he said.

Somehow, I managed to face him. He thumbed the lone tear that escaped my eye.

"I love you, too. True. My leaning on William was out of frustration and that he noticed me when you didn't. But it's you I've always had eyes for. I have love for William, but it's a different kind of love. He's my brother. You know I'm glad we were finally truthful with our feelings. We have a baby coming now, and it's time to step up and fly right for the sake of our child."

"I'm learning how to love you. I've never done love with a woman before," he admitted.

I giggled. It tickled me how he said it. He helped me sit back on the chaise lounge, and we cuddled up and watched a movie until we fell asleep in each other's arms.

Chapter Eighteen

TRUE

Today was Monday, and even though Chance's car accident happened over a week ago on Friday, she assured me she would be okay at home by herself.

"Babe, I have my phone on, and I'll keep it on my hip all day," I told her.

"I'm fine. I won't get up except to use the bathroom, and I'm sure mom will be over later to check on me. I told her to use her key," Chance assured me.

I was a nervous wreck knowing our baby could come at any minute. I headed on to the office after taking Chance downstairs to sit in the theater room. I made sure she had snacks and water nearby, so the only thing she had to get up for was the restroom.

"What up, Will," I sang when I walked in the door.

"True, I didn't expect to see you here today," William commented.

"Man, you know that woman of mine is some kind of superhero," I joked.

William laughed.

"I'm serious. She's taking it like a trooper. If she's in a lot of pain, she's hiding it from me," I said.

"Why doesn't that surprise me," Will scoffed.

"Anyway, man, I'm glad you're here because now that we're alone, I wanted to clear the air with you," I admitted.

"What's up," William asked.

"I apologize, for the bullshit, all of it. My wife and I had a conversation last week. We had a heart to heart, and you and she were a topic of discussion, as well as Lace and the baby. Let me just say we're on a mission to fix our marriage before the baby's born," I told him.

"I'm happy for you," William replied.

I knew this was an awkward topic. I took a deep breath because I knew he was playing me like I didn't know what was going on.

"Listen, man. I just want to thank you for holding my wife up when I was acting an ass," I huffed out.

"Thanks, man, I really do have mad love for Chance. You have a beautiful, intelligent, and business savvy woman, which is what I've tried to tell you the entire time," William acknowledged. He stood up and walked my way and held his hand out for a handshake. I grabbed his hand and then pulled him in for a brotherly hug. We slapped each other's back.

"Thanks for always being my brother over the years," I told him.

"Always," William pounded his chest.

The rest of the morning was uneventful as I poured over purchase orders. It was time to wrap things up for the years end budget.

I called my mother-in-law to see if she stopped by the house to check on Chance.

"Hey mom, did you get to stop by the house," I asked.

"Yes, I'm here now. Chance says she feels fine, but she doesn't look good to me. I'll keep an eye on her. She's sleeping right now," mom said.

"Okay, call me if you need to," I added.

"I will," she said before hanging up the phone.

I sat there, worried. I knew she should have kept that

collar on longer. I kept trying to push through my day, but now I was worried. I grabbed my coat.

"Will, my mother in law said she didn't think Chance was feeling well. I'm out of here for the day. Everything is caught up on my end," I explained.

"No, go on and check on your wife. I got everything under control around here."

"Thanks, man, I owe you," I told him.

"Nah, I'm sure I'll be going through the same thing one day," William laughed.

Traffic was light. I made it home in record time. I pulled the car into the garage and headed into the house.

"Hey, mom. Oh, it smells delicious in here," I said, giving her a half hug and kiss on the cheek.

I hung my coat in the coat closet and washed my hands.

"Chance, hey babe, I'm home. Mom said you weren't feeling well today. What's going on?" I asked.

"I'm cramping really bad in my lower back."

"I'm calling the doctor," I said. "We're not taking any chances."

I had the doctor on speed dial. "Yes, I'm calling about my wife. She is cramping badly in her back, but she was in a car accident a little over a week ago," I explained.

I grabbed Chance's tennis shoes and put them on her feet.

"They told me to bring you in," she had on a pair of sweats and tee-shirt so I grabbed her coat out of the closet. I picked her up and took her out to the car.

"I need to finish up this food, so keep me posted," Mom noted.

"I will," I told her on the way out the door.

I felt terrible because I could see the discomfort in my wife's face as I drove to the doctor's office.

"She's sixty percent effaced and slightly dilated," Doctor Ghiloni explained.

"What does that mean?" I asked.

"Well, it could take a few more days, but this is definitely the beginning!" The doctor exclaimed.

We got back in the car, feeling hopeful with a new rush of excitement.

"Oh my gosh, we're going to be parents soon, True. Are you ready?" Chance asked me.

"I'm scared to death," I cringed in excitement. "What do we do?"

"I guess I should start timing my contractions," she

shrugged.

When we got home, we ate dinner with mom. She was super excited. "I'm going to go home and get my stuff ready, so I can get a little sleep and be prepared for our hospital trip when you guys call."

I helped her into her coat. "I can't stay here because my daughter and I will drive each other crazy," she laughed.

"Don't worry, mom. The doctor said it could take a few more days. You know I won't let you miss anything, and if it's late, I'll send you an Uber. I don't want you driving out there when it gets dark," I added.

"Okay, thank you," mom shut the door behind her.

I sat down next to Chance on the couch, and we took a picture together for Facebook. Chance captioned it saying our special delivery would probably happen this weekend. You know we got a slew of calls after that.

Chelle and Trinity facetimed Chance. "Bitch, are you about to have that baby?"

They all giggled like schoolgirls. I put my Beats on with the music loaded on my phone and laid back for a nap.

Chapter Nineteen

CHANCE

I opened my eyes remembering True said he would run to the office and get his laptop in case he had to work.

These last two weeks of the pregnancy seemed to drag on, but the distinct pain I just felt in my pelvis had me blinking hard. Maybe I had gas or needed to use the restroom. I could hear mom banging around in the kitchen. I peeled myself off the couch, carefully remembering the pains that went dormant when I laid still. I put my collar on when I got up to use the restroom and slowly shuffled to the bathroom, where I sat down to do my business. *That should help*, I thought. I washed my hands and headed back to the theatre room and turned on the TV.

"Hey, sweetie, how are you feeling today?" Mom asked.

"Okay, I guess. I had a little belly ache," I told her.

"Are your contractions getting any closer?" She asked.

"No, I just went to the restroom. I should be okay now. Everything is sitting on my stomach. You know I'm used to moving around. And this heartburn is killing me," I groaned.

"Let me get you a tums," mom headed to the kitchen.

I mindlessly surfed the TV for something to watch. I desperately wanted to get my mind off the discomfort I was experiencing. Minutes later, mom came around the corner with some tea and the container of tums and shook two of them in my palm. I chewed the chalky bites, anxious for them to start working.

"Thanks," I mouthed.

"Let me go in here and finish this food so you and True can have some dinner tonight."

I continued to flip the channels until I stopped at the Lifetime Movie Channel. I never watched this mess, but now I wanted to watch the movies that made me cry. It was a good outlet. I sipped some peppermint tea that mom had made me.

About an hour later, I texted my mom even though she was just in the kitchen. I didn't want to move around unnecessarily. Mom rushed into the theater room.

"Mom, I need to talk through what I'm feeling over here. I'm getting a lot of action."

"It sounds like the baby is moving around in between contractions," Mom said. "Wait, I think I hear the garage door."

"True, bring your wife upstairs and let me run her a hot bath. I think that will help with the pain."

I moaned softly, trying to blow long breaths of air. My lung still hurt, but that pain didn't have anything on the labor pains I was starting to experience.

"I got you, babe," I heard my husband's strong baritone tell me. Once upstairs, he undressed me and placed me down in the large garden tub. The hot water did feel good, and I tried to relax, but I needed to walk.

"I'm ready to get out," I told my husband, who was sitting by my side. He helped pull me to my feet and un-plugged the drain. He dried me off after helping me step over the tub's edge onto the fluffy bathmat.

"True, you don't need to carry me anymore. Bedrest is over. This baby is coming soon, and I need to walk," I told him.

I headed to the bedroom to put on some comfortable lounge clothes. I brushed my hair up into a high ponytail. I walked back into the bathroom and brushed my teeth. I had barely finished when I bent over in agony as I gritted my teeth.

"True, get mom. I need you guys to get my bag packed now," I said with urgency.

It hurt to walk. It hurt to sit, and it hurt to breathe. I couldn't get any relief at all. Tears poured from my eyes.

"Calm down," mom rubbed my back.

"True, get the car backed out. I think we need to get to the hospital," mom instructed.

True grabbed my and the baby's bag and headed down to the car.

"Don't forget the car seat," mom yelled.

I paced the floor during another contraction. Once it was over, I stepped into my Ugg boots and kept walking. True came back with my coat, scarf, and hat before helping me down the stairs with mom on our heels. We got in the car. My body gave me a few restful moments of peace. I closed my eyes and tried to rest.

Soon we were checked in and escorted to our private

birthing room, which looked like a small apartment. Tomorrow was Christmas eve, and it seemed our baby was right on target for the due date. True got busy, making the room comfortable for me. He put on meditation music. The nurse showed him how to read the monitor so he would let me know when a contraction was coming. Mom held the heating pad on my back during the contractions, and they alternated feeding me ice chips and wiping my brow with a cold towel. Because of the neck pain, I didn't mess with the birthing ball.

At one point, True climbed in the bed with me when I tried to take a small nap. Mom loved to snap photos, and I didn't realize she was snapping pictures the whole-time documenting everything. Again, I was up and pacing the floor. I collapsed over the side of the bed in exhaustion.

"It's almost over," True reassuringly told me. All I heard was his baritone. It's what got me through each mounted contraction. This went on all night. When the doctor arrived to examine me at seven a.m., she said I was already dilated to seven centimeters. I couldn't' believe I had been working through the pain. But I couldn't have done it without my husband and mother. I knew this was a different type of pain than I ever experienced, but a needle in my back terrified me even more. Yet, I didn't know how much more I could take. I felt like I was hitting my threshold for pain. The anesthesiologist came into the room to see if I was ready for the epidural.

"I'm scared," I told True.

Doctor Ghiloni examined me again and said I was at eight centimeters.

"Well, what do you want to do? It's only going to get worse," the doctor said. "There could be four or five more hours of contractions like this.

True kissed me on my forehead. "Go with your gut instinct," True said.

"I don't want the epidural," I blurted out.

The doctor and the nurses left the room. Another contraction hit.

"Aaaaaghhhh," I moaned in agony.

"Baby, you're strong. I'm so proud of you." My husband's words fueled my inner strength, and I pushed through each contraction as they became longer and stronger.

My water broke while I was pacing back and forth, and my mother called for someone to clean it up. I didn't feel like I was crying, yet tears were steadily streaming down my face. By the time I reached ten centimeters, there was hardly a break in between contractions. My husband's voice was all I could hear.

"Breathe deeply, in through your nose and blow out," he'd say.

I got chill bumps. After all the time we'd spent together, this was the most intimate. I squeezed his hands as I braced for another contraction. The doctor and nurses rushed back into the room as I got in position to have my baby.

My knees were pulled back, True on one side, mom on the other, and the nurses held my feet.

"Chance with the next contraction, I want you to bear down while I count to ten, release, and then do it again," Doctor Ghiloni told me. "Okay, ten, nine, eight," She counted.

"Aaaaggggghhhh," I gushed and took a quick breath.

"Ten, nine, eight..."

"Aaaaaggghhhhh," I repeated.

Silence came over my body. I could see lips moving, but I didn't know what they were saying.

"I see the head," the doctor said.

"One more good push," True coached.

All I felt at this point was my heart, at the life True, and I created. I sobbed with happiness as they lifted the little body to my chest.

"It's a boy!" Doctor Ghiloni called out.

I was blinded with tears. I felt my mom and husband peppering me with kisses.

I looked down at my baby boy cradled in my arms, sleeping, with True sleeping on the pillow below him. I looked down at my whole world. At that moment, I thanked God for the life he'd given me through my beautiful son. It was at that moment I knew his name was Trance because that was the state he put me in when I saw his handsome face.

I nudged my husband. I hated to wake him because he worked as hard as I did to bring this baby into the world.

"I know his name," I said. "Trance Fury Fourlove."

"I love it." True's smile was more prominent than I'd ever seen before.

"Chance, I love that name. It sounds so strong," mom chimed in.

"Trance is also symbolic of our names merged together, and it means bringer of light," I announced proudly.

Mom snapped our picture and posted it on Facebook so all of our friends would know the baby was here.

The nurses came into the room. "Good morning. We need to take this little guy and run some tests. Why don't you try to get a little sleep while we have the baby?" The nurse suggested.

"I think I will," I responded, suddenly coming down off my adrenaline.

"Babe, I need to run home and shower. Do you mind if I leave for a bit?" True asked.

"No, I don't mind. I'm going to rest for a while. I'm exhausted."

"True, I'm going to ride with you. My car is at your house. Chance, I'll be back up here later this evening," mom said.

"Okay, mom, thanks for everything. I love you," I commented.

"Love you too," mom said.

Chapter Twenty

TRUE

I pulled the car up to the hospital door where mom jumped in. I didn't want her to make the walk across the parking lot.

"Well, True, you're a father. How do you feel?" Mom asked.

"Amazing even though it doesn't feel real yet. I can't wait to get back up there and spend some time with my shorty," I answered.

Mom giggled. "I'm a grandmother," she grinned.

"Yes, you are," I stated in agreement.

I pulled up to a local Tim Horton's drive-through window to grab us both a coffee and a breakfast sandwich that we ate on the ride home.

I dropped mom off in front of my house next to her car. I

made sure she got in. After she pulled off, I pulled into my driveway and the garage.

I ran into the house, took a shower, and plopped down in the bed. I wanted just an hour or two of sleep.

Hours later, I woke up a new man. It was Christmas Eve, and I was anxious to get back to the hospital, but I had a few things to do first. I ran over to Target. I needed decorations. I knew I didn't have much time, so I worked fast, grabbing the essentials. I stopped in the baby department and grabbed a few things for the baby, and in the main aisle, I found exactly what I was looking for.

When I got back to the hospital, Chance was knocked out. All that hard work acted as a sedative putting her into a deep sleep. I tiptoed around the room, putting my plan into action. I looked around. Everything was perfect. I went into the bathroom to get changed, and then I went to the nursery to get my beautiful son.

The nurse scanned each of our bands to ensure I was the right parent getting the right baby. I asked the nurse to help me put the outfit I'd bought Trance to wear on Christmas Eve, and she was happy to help.

"You guys are so cute," the nurse cooed.

I pushed the baby to the room in his bassinette, and as hard as Chance had been sleeping, she woke up immediately when she heard him.

She pushed the button to raise the bed.

"Whaaat in the world! True," she squealed.

I watched her eyes as they scanned the room. She saw the four-foot decorated Christmas tree complete with gifts under it sitting in the corner. I had lights on it strung around the window.

"You and Trance have on matching Christmas pajamas. You guys are so adorable," Chance commented.

I grabbed a box from up under the tree, careful not to drop Trance, and brought it over to Chance.

"Remember how you said your father would always allow you to open one gift on Christmas Eve?" I asked.

"Yeah?"

"Well, here's your one gift," I smiled as she ripped it open.

"Awe," she choked, matching Christmas pajamas like you and Trance." I placed the baby in the bassinette. After pulling the hospital gown off Chance, I helped her into the long tee with the same print. I picked the baby back up and brought him to her.

"True, he has your dimples," she sang.

I beamed with pride. I smirked and rubbed my goatee.

"You are too much," she laughed.

I climbed back in the bed with her, and we posed for a selfie that I posted on Facebook.

"Look who came home for Christmas," was the caption. We sat there for hours, pouring love into our new bundle of joy. Then there was a tap at the door.

"Come in," Chance said.

The curtain was pulled back so we couldn't see who it was, but then we heard.

"Silent Night Holy Night," being sung. It sounded like a whole choir. I got out of the bed and pulled the curtain back. It was all of our friends standing there holding candles and caroling. Some of the nurses on the floor were gathered in the back singing along too. Mom, Trinity, Chelle, Zen, 'O', William, Steal, Kelvin, and Brian our whole circle of friends, our family.

"Merry Christmas," they all said.

"I can't believe you guys brought Christmas to me," Chance cried. "I have never cried so much in my whole life.

Everyone piled in the room one by one to see the baby.

"Big Will," I said, hugging my bro.

"Man, what are these soft ass pajamas you're wearing," Will joked. "Yeah, you are officially a dad," he chuckled.

The nurse came into the room. "Merry Christmas, everyone. We broke the rules allowing you all in together, but visiting hours are over in five minutes," she explained.

We all took a few photos together. The nurse even took one of all of us. After everyone left, I kissed my wife.

"I love you, dearly, thank you for giving me a son," I said to Chance.

"I love you too, and boy, didn't I tell you I was tired of crying."

"Merry Christmas, my loves," I whispered.

The End!

Thanks, for reading. Please leave a review if you enjoyed this story to helps others find my books.

Also, by Amber Ghe:

The Mergers & Acquisitions Series:
Mergers & Acquisitions
Game Faces On
Dreams Under Construction

The Dream Series:
To Steal a Dream

Christmas Chance:

Mixfits Series:
Mixfits

Bliss Way Short Stories:
Bliss Way
Candid for You
Love Makes Scents (free)

ABOUT THE AUTHOR

Amber Ghe

 Amber Ghe is the author of the compelling series' Mergers and Acquisitions.' Writing about characters who examine their lives, their hopes, fears, and motivations, characters that will linger with you long after the story is over. She dreams that one day, the Mergers & Acquisitions series will become an internet series or motion picture.

Co-Authoring the exhilarating book 'Diary of a Ready Woman,' she's made it her mission to encourage healthy self-esteem, attitude, and woman empowerment. Turning her daily mantra into her upcoming book, Girl, 'Show up for Your Life!' she's decided to make that her movement. A jack of all trades, she loves to dabble in art, design, movies, and of course, reading.

Working a nine-to-five by day and author by night, she hopes to one day make it a full-time job.

She currently resides in Ohio with her husband, where she is a full-time mom. She's following her real passion by working on her next novels.

FOLLOW ME

@https://linktr.ee/booksbyamberg

Made in the USA
Columbia, SC
19 November 2020

24883584R00083